S0-ACN-133

HEART OF THE MOUNTAINS

HEART OF THE MOUNTAINS

•

Karen Cogan

AVALON BOOKS
NEW YORK

Published by Avalon Books,
an imprint of Thomas Bouregy & Co., Inc.
160 Madison Avenue, New York, NY 10016

Library of Congress Cataloging-in-Publication Data

Cogan, Karen.
  Heart of the mountains / Karen Cogan.
        p. cm.
  ISBN 978-0-8034-7607-3 (hardcover : acid-free
paper) 1. Family secrets—Fiction. 2. Colorado—
Fiction.   I. Title.
  PS3603.O325H43 2011
  813'.6—dc22

                                    2011018712

PRINTED IN THE UNITED STATES OF AMERICA
ON ACID-FREE PAPER
BY RR DONNELLEY, BLOOMSBURG, PENNSYLVANIA

Chapter One

Spring sunshine poured from a cloudless turquoise sky, warming Deborah Palmer's shoulders as she stepped off the train. She glanced around, her brown eyes anxiously scanning the groups of people milling around the depot. Her aunt's letter had promised that her uncle would be here to meet her. Yet the promise had given her small comfort when the train had pulled into this narrow canyon surrounded by towering peaks. Her aunt was a stranger to her, as was her uncle. She would not be able to pick him out in a crowd.

She pushed back her round straw hat and took a few steps forward along the wooden platform. She clutched her worn cloth valise as though her life depended upon it, though in truth she had nothing of value packed inside.

A short, stoutly built man climbed slowly down from a wagon and ambled toward the depot. He approached Deborah and paused. "You must be my niece, Deborah. I've been sent to fetch you."

As she was a good inch taller, she stared down into his eyes. "Uncle Pete?"

He tilted his hat back, exposing his balding head. "That's me. I would have known you anywhere. You're tall, like your aunt. And you have the same brown eyes and hair. Only you're skinnier. She'll want to fatten you up."

Deborah tucked a stray wisp of hair behind her ear and decided that the women in her family must share the same tall, sturdy build. Even her little sister, Mary Lynn, was showing signs of growing into her long legs.

She shook off her thoughts of home, not wanting to dwell on being a robust farm girl. While she was growing up in Kansas, she assumed she'd be tall like her ma. The thought had never bothered her. She'd never thought it would matter. Yet now, she felt sure that it had played a part in the humiliating betrayal that was one of the reasons she had come to Ouray.

She followed her uncle to the wagon. By the time she climbed onto the seat, she was out of breath. She felt her temples pounding and knew she was not in Kansas anymore. It was going to take a day or two to get used to the altitude.

Pete turned the wagon around. "Let's pull up beside the train and load your bags."

Deborah nodded. "I appreciate your taking me in like this and giving me a job."

He pulled the wagon to a stop beside the baggage car. There was already a pile of belongings on the ground. He gave Deborah a lopsided grin. "You'll earn your keep with your Aunt Carrie, you know. She's a firm believer in hard work."

Like my ma, no doubt, Deborah thought a bit dourly.

Yet she smiled at her uncle and said, "I was raised on a farm. I'm used to hard work."

She pointed out the two moth-eaten bags that contained the remainder of her clothing. Pete hoisted them into the wagon. The bags were new when Ma had used them as a bride. Now the striped fabric was faded, and the wooden handles were cracked. With the characteristic hardness that was part of Ma now, and the cynicism that Deborah could no longer stand, Ma had parted with the bags without the slightest sentimental attachment.

"I won't be needing these again," she'd said as she flung them onto Deborah's bed. "I intend to live and die without leaving this farm."

Again Deborah pulled her mind away from thoughts of home. The last thing she wanted to do was remember her shattered plans. Nearly all her life, she had planned on a future with Timothy. She had spent hours, when she was milking cows or hoeing the garden, wondering what it would be like to be his wife. It had seemed as settled as the sunrise each morning. A fact of life. His love would rescue her from a life she had grown to hate, toiling from dawn to dusk on a dirt farm while listening to Ma's criticism day and night. Even on the rare occasion they got a little money ahead from garden or egg sales, Ma refused to make any changes that would make life easier for herself and her girls. Little things—like getting a bar of store-bought soap instead of stirring a pot of hot lye, or new material for a dress for Mary Lynn when her old ones were obviously too short—were forbidden. Her sister had no shoes for the summer. Ma bought shoes for her only in the winter. If Mary Lynn outgrew them before the next winter, she went without. Deborah didn't mind so much for herself, but she hated to see Mary Lynn self-conscious about her clothes and lack of shoes.

When her plans with Timothy were pulled from her so unexpectedly, there seemed to be nothing to keep her in Kansas. Her home life was unhappy, and she had no other beau. She had to find a place where she would not feel hollow inside, like an empty shell. She wanted to make a new start. And since the only place she had relatives was Ouray, she came here.

And now she was facing life in a new town, completely removed from everything in her past. Though she felt adrift, she was determined to make a new life for herself. She was a hard worker. She would earn her keep, and maybe even her own business one day.

On the way to the boardinghouse that Carrie and Pete owned, Deborah glanced around, intrigued by the differences between her farming community and this mining town. Victorian buildings lined the streets. In spite of the animosity she felt at being exiled here, she had to admit to being impressed by the dignified stone structures, so different from the wood-and-sod buildings in their closest hamlet in Kansas.

As they plodded through town, the late-afternoon sun cast a fiery glow onto the mountains to the south. Deborah squinted at the imposing sentinels and asked, "What makes that mountain so red?"

Pete followed her gaze and said, "That's Red Mountain. They're actually three mountains. Iron pyrite, fools' gold, makes them look red. They're the home of the Yankee Girl Mine. I wish I could have been John Robinson and discovered it. He took out a thousand ounces of silver per ton of ore."

He clicked his tongue. "I'd have been a rich man by now."

Deborah nodded, though she was completely ignorant about the worth of silver. If the subject had been the season for planting wheat or how to treat a sick cow, she would have felt more in her element. At least she knew how to cook and sew and clean. She would not be useless at the boardinghouse.

As they crossed onto the bridge at Seventh Street, Deborah gaped down at the river, whose water rushed swiftly along, as though it were hurrying to an important task. She turned to her uncle and said, "It runs right through town?"

"Yep. It's handy to have water close by. It's full of snowmelt right now. Makes it act sassy."

Deborah had never heard a river described quite like that, but this one did seem to have a will of its own. She tried to figure out which mountain was its source but lost track of it as they left the bridge and lumbered onto a street with a number of shops and a fancy-looking hotel. On this Friday afternoon the streets were crowded with the horses and mules that were tied at the hitching rails. Men and women wove among them, coming and going amid the shops like a colony of ants conducting business.

"This is a busy place," Deborah observed.

Pete nodded. "Me and Carrie have seen Ouray bust and seen her spring back after gold was found at Camp Bird Mine. There's a lot of fine families in Ouray. I reckon me and Carrie will be here come whatever."

Deborah had once felt that sense of belonging in her small community in Kansas. That was why she had balked at leaving the only home she'd known. Yet now that she was here, her curiosity was piqued. In spite of her natural reserve, she felt excited by the sights and sounds of a new beginning. Perhaps it was just what she needed to rouse her from the disappointment that had claimed her these last few weeks.

Pete chewed on a piece of straw as he pulled his two horses to a stop in front of a square-fronted house that sported the sign CARRIE'S BOARDINGHOUSE. It was painted the color of burned sugar and had blue trim. In the front yard, lupines and laurel were already in bloom.

She climbed from the wagon and took her valise while Pete lugged the two bags to the house. She nodded to an old man with thinning white hair who sat sunning himself on the porch. He stared back with interest.

"Who you got there, Pete?"

Raising his voice, Pete answered, "This is my niece, Deborah Palmer. She's come to stay here and help at the boardinghouse. It'll work out good for us. I've been telling Carrie for the last couple years she isn't getting any younger."

The old man chuckled. "She does buzz around, just like a bee."

Pete told Deborah, "This is Joe Greene. He was a miner before he became a long-time resident here."

Deborah smiled at the old man. "Nice to meet you, Mr. Greene."

Joe fixed Deborah with a puzzled look. "You say it's time to eat with you? Seems kind of early to me."

Pete chuckled. "Joe's a little hard of hearing."

He shouted to Joe, "She says it's nice to meet you."

Joe's face, wrinkled and brown as a walnut, creased into a smile. "Oh, nice to meet you too. And let me know when it's time for supper. I'd be pleased to eat with you."

Pete stifled a grin as he steered Deborah inside. "When

he gets an idea into his head, especially one he likes, you'll never get it out."

A small parlor lay to the left of the entry hall. Deborah glanced around the room. It was nicely furnished, with an armchair and a cowhide-covered sofa. A small table with a fancy lamp sat between them. A bright, sunny window faced the street, and a gleaming piano, obviously the pride of the room, sat against the wall.

She turned as she heard a woman say, "Is that my niece? Let me have a look at you."

A large-boned woman wiped her hands on her apron as she rushed toward Deborah. If Deborah hadn't already known that her mother had a sister, she could have guessed it now. Carrie's gray-streaked chestnut hair was pulled up in a topknot. Several strands had escaped and curled willfully toward her face. Her dark eyes that turned up slightly at the corners shone with interest as she paused only inches in front of Deborah. "My, my, here she is, little Deborah. I've never even seen you, though I knew your Pa well when he stayed here to work his mine. You look just like your mother, or like she did when she was your age."

Deborah could not remember ever having been called "little" in her life. It gave her a homey feeling to be fussed over and welcomed as family. She decided at once that she liked this large, boisterous woman. No matter how demanding she might prove to be, she had a liveliness that Deborah's mother had lost in the years since Pa had gone away.

"It was kind of you to let me come. I'll try hard to be a help to you."

Carrie threw back her head and laughed. "I'm the one who got the good deal, and don't you forget it. A fine strong girl to help me with the heavy work is just what I've been needing."

She took Deborah by the elbow. "Bring her bags, Pete. We'll show her to her room. She'll be tired and hungry after such a long trip."

Deborah grabbed one bag while Pete obligingly picked up the other and trod behind them up the stairs that led straight up to the second floor. They were narrow, with a gold-colored woolen runner to give them a cultured touch.

"You have a nice place," Deborah observed.

Carrie looked back over her shoulder at her niece. "It's not the Beaumont. But we do our best to keep it neat and clean."

"The Beaumont?"

"A fancy hotel here in town. It has three floors and a grand staircase that divides at the landing, just like a wishbone."

Deborah had never been in a fine hotel—or any hotel, for that matter. She could hardly imagine what it must look like inside. But, of course, it was for people who could afford such opulence. She could never feel comfortable in such a fine place and was glad she was in a boardinghouse instead.

Carrie halted in front of a door at the end of the hall. She pushed it open and stepped aside so that Deborah could enter. The room was small and square and neat as a pin. The bed was made up with a cheerful patchwork quilt of blue and gold. The bedside table held a clock and a vase of wildflowers. Blue-checked gingham curtains hung at a window that overlooked the street.

Pete set her bag upon the braided rug that warmed the

polished wooden floor and said, "I hope you'll be comfortable."

"I'm sure I will. It's lovely, so bright and fresh."

In Kansas, she'd shared a bedroom in a drafty farmhouse with Mary Lynn. It was dingy, with one lumpy mattress and a faded cotton blanket. The roof leaked when it rained, and the floor was rough and splintered. And that was the way it would stay, since there were never enough money or hands available to do any repairs.

Carrie pointed to a tall wardrobe that sat against the wall. "You can put all your things in there."

Deborah nodded. "I'll have more than enough room."

Carrie looked pleased by Deborah's approval of the room. She pushed a lock of hair behind her ear and said, "We'll leave you to rest awhile. Supper is at six o'clock sharp." She nodded toward the clock. "Make sure you're down on time."

"I will."

Showing up late would, no doubt, earn a reproof. Though Carrie had a kind manner, Deborah could tell that she was firm in her rules. And Deborah didn't need reminding that the condition of her remaining here was that she remember that Carrie was not only her aunt but also her employer.

"I'll be downstairs seeing to supper if you need me," Carrie said.

She closed the door, leaving Deborah to her own devices for the hour before the meal. Deborah sank onto the bed, took off her shoes, and stretched her toes. A shaft of sunlight fell across her legs, warming the skin under her dark stockings.

She sat awhile, enjoying the luxury of being all alone in such a pleasant room. Soon she would be thrown into the busy routine of early rising to cook and scrub and bake. For this one hour, she could relish the feeling of being a guest in her aunt's home, and she intended to enjoy every moment of it.

Still, after a short time she grew restless. She'd never been allowed to indulge in idleness. With the exception of the few times she'd been sick, she couldn't remember ever sitting around with nothing to do. And she had much to do now, she reminded herself. It would be smart to get her clothes put away before she came back to her room after supper, dead tired from her travel.

She pulled open the door to the wardrobe. The faint smell of mothballs drifted from its dark depths. She was pleased to find that it was roomy enough to hold all her belongings with room to spare.

She opened her bags and began to pull out her dresses and petticoats. After three days on the train, they looked as limp and rumpled as she felt. Still, she shook them out and arranged them carefully to smooth out the wrinkles. She saved room on the bottom of the wardrobe for the few books that she had managed to collect over the years. Most of them had belonged to her father. She carried them in her pockets and read any time she could sneak a few moments away from her chores.

She ran her fingers lovingly over the leather-bound cover of *Pilgrim's Progress*. It had belonged to her father when he was a boy. Carrie had sent it back along with his other belongings when he'd disappeared from Ouray. Her mother had shown no interest in his possessions and raised no objections when Deborah had claimed the books.

He had stayed here, in this very house, perhaps even in this room. She sighed, wondering again what had happened to him. She had not seen him since she was a little girl. Had he really run away with a saloon girl, as rumor had it, or had he met some other fate? Though she'd never expected to live in Ouray, perhaps now that she was here she could find some clue that would set her mind at rest. For in all these years, she had never forgotten him.

She remembered how he had carried her on his shoulders when she met him coming home from plowing the fields. No matter how long he'd been out in the sun, his gray eyes always sparkled when he saw her. "Deborah, my bonny girl," he had said when he swung her into his arms. In the evenings, he had played his fiddle and sung for them. She and her brothers had danced while her mother looked up from her mending and smiled.

And then he went away to seek their fortune in silver, and the happy times had ended. Ma had argued and pleaded with him, all to no avail. He had been sure that he would return rich enough to expand their farm and livestock.

Deborah had cried for days. Yet he did not return. And as the months passed, Ma's expression grew ever more pinched and her tongue more sharp. The house grew quiet, and the family grew morose. Even the scrawny tabby that had taken to sitting on their porch stopped coming around.

Then that terrible letter came saying that Pa hadn't come back to the boardinghouse and that some of the miners had drifted off to California. The family waited, hoping that Pa was on his way home. But as the days became months, hope faded, and they were forced to accept that he was not coming home.

Life settled into a routine. The boys handled the field

work with occasional help from Deborah and her ma. The women tended to the house and gardens, and though money was tight they managed to survive.

She shook off these painful memories and closed the wardrobe. Drawn by the bright sunlight, she ambled over to the window to look down at the street. She smiled at the comforting scene of women leading children by the hand and men hurrying home for supper. She could see that her aunt had been truthful when she wrote that Ouray was a family town full of honest and hard-working citizens.

Only one area of town catered to the baser instincts of citizens who frequented the cribs and saloons, on Second Street between Seventh and Eighth Avenues. This gave Deborah comfort, since she'd heard that some mining towns drew only the lowest sorts of violent men and brazen women.

Perhaps in this clean and attractive town she would one day feel at home. Even if she didn't, it couldn't be worse than remaining in Kansas and enduring the disgrace of being jilted by a childhood beau.

She turned from the window and glanced at the clock. The time had flown by, leaving her only fifteen minutes to wash her face and hands and unsnarl the tangles from her hair. She would have to hurry, for she didn't dare be late.

She unclasped the tortoiseshell clip that held her hair and began to brush through the tangles. She grimaced with each snag but continued with determination until her hair fell in a smooth, silky sheen atop her shoulders. She studied herself in the oval wall mirror as she gathered up her hair on each side of her head and fastened it in the clip.

She gave her bangs scant attention and then dropped the brush onto the bedside table.

She washed at the basin and dried herself on a towel that smelled of fresh air and rose hips. She hugged it to her face and breathed deeply of the fragrance. Everything about this room was clean and cheerful. It would be her haven, no matter how tired she might be after each day. She would look forward to coming here and closing her door, shutting herself away from the world. Here, no one would judge her, and she would have peace.

She harbored no silly dreams for her future. She asked only for a roof over her head, daily meals, and a little time for her books. That would be enough.

She straightened the dainty lace collar on her dress and headed down to supper. In the hall other boarders were stirring from their rooms. She exchanged greetings with a young man who allowed her to precede him down the stairs. He had dark hair that was parted severely in the middle, a sparse mustache, and round spectacles that gave his face an owlish look. He was slight of build and did not fill out his white shirt and woolen trousers.

"Allow me to introduce myself. I'm Oscar Evans. I work for the newspaper."

"It's nice to meet you, Mr. Evans. I'm Deborah Palmer. I've come to work for my aunt."

She paused at the bottom of the stairs to extend her hand. Oscar grasped it enthusiastically. "Call me Oscar. And it would be my pleasure to show you around town. I could fill you in on all that's happening."

Deborah stared down at him. "That's very kind of you, Oscar, but I don't know when I'll have the time. I'll have a lot of duties around the boardinghouse."

"Maybe some evening when we've both finished work. I cover meetings and concerts at the Wright Opera House. We could take in a concert or see a play."

Since he was not put off by the two inches that she towered above him, it was obvious that young Oscar was not going to be easily dissuaded. She would have to think of a means to keep this overeager man at bay.

She smiled at him. "I'll have to talk to my aunt. She may not think it's a good idea for me to keep company with the residents."

He gave her a conspiratorial wink as he took her by the elbow to escort her to the dining room. "You leave that to me. I know how to handle Carrie."

Deborah stifled a laugh. She doubted that he had Carrie wrapped around his scrawny little finger. Unless she missed her guess, it was Carrie who knew how to handle Oscar.

They arrived just as Carrie set a plate of fluffy white biscuits on a long oak table that was piled high with roast beef, string beans, and potatoes. Deborah excused herself from Oscar to see if she could help Carrie.

Carrie shook her head. "Not tonight. Tonight you rest up. Tomorrow, you work."

Carrie pointed to a chair at the end of the table. "I've put out an extra chair. You can eat in here tonight and get to know everybody."

Old Joe Greene arrived and set up a fuss. He scowled at the two gentlemen seated on each side of his chair and said, "One of you will have to move. She promised to have supper with me."

Carrie stepped in and said, "You come down here, Joe.

There's room beside Deborah at the end of the table if everyone moves down one seat."

By the time she'd repeated it two more times, Joe was happily enthroned beside Deborah, who would have preferred to eat anywhere except amid this group of strangers. By the time they began to pass the food, she was being peppered with questions about her background, mostly from Oscar Evans. About her past, all she would tell them was that she had wanted to leave the farm to live in a town.

Old Joe came to her rescue, asking so often what was being said that they gave up questioning her. Instead, Joe grilled her. "You ever been in these parts before?"

"No, but my father lived here years ago. He worked a mine claim for a while."

Joe's bushy brow went up in interest. "What was your pa's name?"

"Ed Palmer."

His faded old eyes widened before he looked away. He became so quiet that Deborah hoped he hadn't become sick.

"Did you know my father?"

He didn't seem to hear her. She asked again and he shook his head. Of course, it was impossible, with Joe, to know if he had understood what she said.

Nonetheless, he sent her several sidelong glances during the rest of the meal. Yet he didn't say another word. Since she didn't know what to make of his sudden reserve, she simply enjoyed being able to eat in peace.

Carrie brought out a cherry pie with fresh whipped cream, and in spite of her discomfort with her company, Deborah didn't remember when she had enjoyed a meal more. At home on the farm, meals were usually hectic to get on the table and accompanied by either quarreling or silent exhaustion.

After supper, she was determined to help Carrie clean up. Her aunt wouldn't hear of it. "Now you shoo. I told you that you could do as you pleased tonight. You best enjoy it, because it won't happen again."

Oscar jumped on the opportunity like a duck on a beetle. "You wouldn't mind if Deborah took a walk around town with me, would you? I'd like to show her the sights."

Carrie had time only to raise her brows before Deborah rushed to say, "Thanks for the offer, but my traveling has made me too tired. All I want is a bath and a quiet evening in my room."

Oscar looked disappointed. He adjusted his glasses and said, "We can do it another time."

He turned to Carrie. "You have no objection if I show her round town when she's not so tired, do you?"

Carrie began to collect the dishes. The other tenants had already drifted away from the table. "As long as it's not on my time."

Oscar beamed.

Deborah excused herself and plodded up the stairs to her room. She would have to talk to her aunt. But now she intended to grab fresh clothes and find the room that held the tub. She would chain the door and soak until she felt like going back to her room to read. And she would hope that tomorrow she could discourage Oscar. Perhaps then her problems with men would be resolved.

Chapter Two

Deborah snuggled deeper under the quilt as the first rays of dawn filled the room with pale light. She stretched her legs and was surprised not to feel Mary Lynn's gangly limbs beside her. She decided she must have overslept and that Mary Lynn had gotten up without waking her. Ma would be annoyed.

She opened her eyes and looked around. She blinked, trying to remember when she had gotten gingham curtains and a polished wardrobe. Then she remembered that she was no longer on the farm. She was in Ouray now, and she was here to help Carrie, not lollygag in bed.

She glanced nervously at the clock and sighed with relief. Her years of rising with the sun had not failed her. She had not overslept. It was only five thirty, plenty of time to dress and help with the breakfast that would be served in an hour.

She threw back the covers and swung her feet onto the braided rug. She pulled on her petticoat before slipping into a paisley dress that was somewhat faded from wear.

17

Then she brushed her fluffy hair and clasped it on each side in an attempt to restrain it.

The house was still quiet as she slipped downstairs. Carrie was already in the kitchen, mixing dough for biscuits. She gave Deborah a nod of approval. "I'm glad you're punctual. I like that in a person. You can start frying the bacon while I finish this dough."

Deborah took an apron from the hook beside the door and tied it around her dress. Then she took the thick slices of bacon and set them to cook in two massive iron skillets that were already on the stove. As it sizzled, she turned it with a fork and asked, "What else will we be fixing?"

"I'll start oatmeal when I get the biscuits in, and you can scramble the eggs when the bacon's done. That's what we serve every day of the week except Sunday. On Sunday, I serve stacks of flapjacks and bacon."

Carrie pointed a floury hand toward a row of neat shelves that held the dishes. "You can set the table for six. Just don't forget to watch the bacon."

Deborah carried the plates and utensils out to the table. She opened the curtains and let a shaft of sunlight fill the room. Then she set about her task. When the table was all set, she hurried back to the kitchen and was greeted by the sweet aroma of biscuits and the meaty smell of bacon.

Lured by the scent, her stomach awoke and demanded a share. She would have to ignore its request until everyone else was fed, for she was not a guest today. And she was glad of that, if it meant she'd escape taking her meals with Oscar.

When the boarders arrived, she served them breakfast with quiet efficiency. Old Joe did not ask her to sit with him. In fact, he ignored her completely, not meeting her eyes or speaking to her. She didn't spend much time wondering about the change in him. She was too glad that he wasn't paying her any mind. She had enough to do with fending off Oscar, who kept pestering her to take a walk with him when she finished her work that evening.

She managed a vague excuse to postpone taking up his invitation and then sighed with relief when he hurried off to work. The other boarders left as well, and she began to clear the dishes. She blew a strand of hair off her face as she carried the stack of plates into the kitchen.

Carrie had a tub of hot, sudsy water ready. Deborah set the dishes to soak and joined Carrie for breakfast. Carrie grinned as she stabbed a slice of bacon for herself. "That Oscar still asking to show you around?"

"Yes. And since I don't want to take up with him, I've been meaning to ask you not to let me consort with your boarders. Then I could refuse him without hurting his feelings. He'd figure it was your rule."

Carrie nodded. "If that's how you feel, I'd be glad for you to tell him I don't want you mingling with my tenants. If you were to have a lover's quarrel, it might make things unpleasant around here."

Deborah shivered. "I don't have any intention of having a lover's quarrel with him or anyone else."

"Old Joe seemed sweet on you too."

"Until dinner last night. I must have said something to offend him. He didn't say a word to me at breakfast this morning."

Carrie laughed. "I'm surprised he heard anything you said."

Deborah looked thoughtful as she tried to remember the conversation. "He asked Pa's name and then got real quiet. Do you suppose he knew Pa?"

"Could have. He's been here a long time. He lived next to his mine back in those days."

"Maybe I'll ask him about Pa. I've never felt easy in my mind about what happened to him."

"Me either. I always figured his partner, Roy Taylor, murdered him for his share of the silver. I never trusted Roy. Most folks didn't, especially after he disappeared too."

"You knew his partner?"

"Not well. But I know he didn't care a fiddlestick about his wife and little boy."

"Maybe Joe could tell me about him."

"It don't hurt to ask."

They finished breakfast and set about cleaning up the kitchen. Deborah washed the dishes, and Carrie stored the food. After they finished, Carrie said, "I'll start cleaning rooms if you'll run down to the butcher shop and get us some meat for supper stew. I'll tell you how to find the shop. It's not far."

Deborah felt anxious at the thought of venturing from her cozy nest. Still, it might be exciting to have a walk through town. She could get an idea of the goods and services offered in Ouray. Though Carrie probably hoped Deborah would take over the running of the boarding-house someday, Deborah felt she'd rather own a little shop of her own, maybe a small bakery where she would make cakes and pies.

If she was successful, she could still board with Carrie. She felt a pang of regret at the thought of spending the rest of her life living alone in one small room. She had never imagined herself without Timothy. If things had worked out for her in Kansas, she would have had a home of her own by now.

She pushed aside her brooding thoughts and listened as Carrie gave directions to the butcher shop. It was only a couple of blocks. She could be there and back in less than a half hour.

Deborah pulled on her bonnet and grabbed a shawl. She'd already found that mornings and evenings could be quite cool. She supposed she shouldn't be surprised, considering the elevation. In this box canyon they were surrounded by snow-blanketed mountains. The view from her bedroom window was breathtaking. Yet with all that whiteness it would be a while before it truly felt like late spring.

She followed the path from the boardinghouse down to the street. It was springing to life with the coming and going of buggies, the shouts of children as they called to one another, and shopkeepers opening their doors.

She passed a lovely Victorian house, painted blue, with a neat picket fence in the yard. She passed a dry goods store where the wiry shopkeeper paused from sweeping his front step to give her a nod and greeting. And at the corner of Fifth and Main, she stood gawking at the impressive Beaumont Hotel. Now that she was standing face-to-face with the incredible structure, she could understand why her aunt had laughed at the comparison to the boardinghouse.

If the sign had not said that it was a hotel, she would have thought it was a palace. Its graceful, arched windows looked down on the street, while its towering steeples reached toward the clear blue sky. She was so entranced, she could have stared for hours. Yet she remembered that she worked for her aunt now and was not on her own time. With a sigh, she turned away and prepared to cross the street.

She didn't notice the tall, blond-haired man who walked out of the sheriff's office. But Jake made it his business to know everybody in Ouray. And he knew that the tall, shapely, dark-haired woman who stood on the corner was either new here or just passing through.

Jake had grown up in Ouray. He knew this town. He was fast with a gun, and he knew how to handle the trouble-makers who frequented the parlor houses and cribs. When it came time for him to decide on a job, it had seemed natural for him to stay and become the sheriff.

As he scanned the street, taking deep breaths of the frosty morning air, he kept his eye on the woman. Most likely she was a guest at the hotel and would be in town for only a few days. Jake had not yet met a woman to his liking. He wanted a woman of substance, one who wouldn't be destroyed by the hardships of life. The small, helpless types were not for him. This woman looked like she could stand on her own two feet.

In less than a heartbeat, his musing turned to quick action. The woman was staring behind her at the hotel while she walked into the street straight into the path of a rapidly approaching Concord stagecoach. Six horses rattled toward her as she jerked alert and froze.

Jake sprang from the opposite corner and, with surprising speed for such a big man, closed the distance between them. He hurled himself toward her and without slowing his pace grasped her around the waist and carried them both safely back to the boardwalk.

The stagecoach pounded past as Jake set her down. She stared up at him, eyes wide and startled. He looked down into those dark eyes and saw that they were the color of rich coffee. His gaze dropped to her lips, which were full and blood red and parted slightly in surprise.

He was panting from exertion. He let go of her and said, "It pays to watch where you're going when you step into a street."

His fear on her behalf made his tone sharper than he'd intended.

Deborah stared up at the giant who had manhandled her to safety at the corner of the Beaumont. She was still trying to make sense of what had happened when his chastising words penetrated her shock. Any gratitude that she might have felt evaporated in a flood of self-justification. It was not as though she had been trying to walk into danger. She had glanced down the street before she started across and had looked behind her for only a moment.

She pulled herself up to look him square in the eye. "I do look where I'm going. I can assure you this is the first time I've ever stepped in front of a stage."

He held her in the penetrating gaze of a schoolmaster with a wayward pupil. His eyes were very blue, and he had a narrow nose that gave him a look of authority. He had a firm chin with a cleft in the center and short sandy hair that barely showed beneath his Stetson hat.

For the first time, Deborah noticed the badge pinned to his chest. She sucked in a sharp breath and said, "You're the sheriff."

For a few fearful heartbeats, she wondered if he might arrest her.

Then he smiled and said, "I am. Name's Jake Taylor."

He quirked a sandy brow and asked, "Are you staying at the hotel?"

"No. I'm living with my aunt."

"Who would that be?"

"Carrie Turner. She owns a boardinghouse down Fifth Street."

Jake nodded. "I know the place. I didn't know she had a niece."

"She does. My name is Deborah Palmer. My aunt sent me to fetch meat for supper stew. If I don't get on my way soon, she'll wonder what's happened to me."

She disliked having to ask permission from him to be on her way, yet he didn't look like the sort of man who would let her turn her back and walk away. Besides, he had saved her life. A twinge of conscience made her add, a bit stiffly, "I do thank you for pulling me from the path of that coach."

Jake tipped his hat. "Be careful on the way back. I'd hate for all that effort to go wasted if you stepped right in front of another buggy."

Deborah's eyes sparked, wondering if it was an insult. She knew she was big, but he hadn't seemed worn out by pulling her to safety. "I'm sorry to have put you to so much trouble. I can assure you it won't happen again."

She stalked away after a careful look down the street. Jake stared after her, amusement at the feisty newcomer shining in his eyes.

Deborah stifled the urge to look back at the sheriff. With her luck, she'd step right in front of a runaway buggy, and at her funeral, he'd tell the whole town that he'd warned her to be careful.

She could still feel his hands around her waist. They were big hands that spanned around her as though she were dainty. He must be at least six feet tall, because she remembered looking up into his eyes. They were an intense blue, as blue as the sky overhead. In spite of her wish to not have noticed it, Sheriff Taylor was a very handsome man.

She found the butcher shop, opened the screen door, and stepped inside. The interior seemed dim after the bright sunshine. A fly buzzed past her face, and she wrinkled her nose. Even on the farm, she'd never liked the smell of fresh meat.

She stood in line at the meat counter behind a woman who held a little girl with soft brown curls. The child looked over her mother's shoulder and gave Deborah a shy smile. Deborah grinned back. She could remember when Mary Lynn was that age and Deborah had carried her sister in her arms. She'd grown up so quickly. And this little girl would too.

The mother finished her purchase and turned with her package, nearly colliding with Deborah. She stared up from her petite height, flushing as she apologized. "I'm sorry. I didn't know you'd come in."

"It's all right. I've been standing here making friends with your little girl."

"She must like you. She can be very shy with strangers."

"I just got here yesterday, so I'm certainly a stranger."

The woman raised a feathery brow. "Really? Where are you from?"

"A farm in Kansas. I've come to help my aunt, Carrie Turner, at her boardinghouse."

"I've met Carrie, though I don't know her well. My name is Nancy Parker. And this is my daughter, Kathleen."

Kathleen hid her face in her mother's collar and they both laughed.

"It's nice to meet you both. I'm Deborah Palmer."

Nancy smiled. "I'm going toward the boardinghouse. Maybe we could walk along and chat when you've bought what you need."

"I'd like that. I only need some meat for supper stew."

When the butcher had wrapped her meat, Deborah thanked him and walked out with Nancy. She was glad to be back in the sunshine and fresh air. She shifted her shawl to hang at her elbows. The day was warming nicely. The sun caressed her face as she lifted it up to soak in the rays.

"I don't think I've ever seen a sky so clear or so blue," she said.

"I hadn't either until I came to Silverton, and then to Ouray," Nancy said.

"It must be very cold here in the winter."

"It is. And there's a lot of snow. But we had plenty of supplies last winter and a nice snug house. It wasn't too bad. Still, I wouldn't want to do much winter traveling again. I was terrified of avalanches when we were on the toll road to get here."

"An avalanche?"

"You know, when the snow shakes loose from a mountain. Several men got buried in one this past year. It took days before they were found."

Deborah shuddered. "It sounds terrible."

They reached the corner across from the Beaumont Hotel. Deborah's pulse jumped as she scanned the street to see if Jake was still there. She didn't know whether she felt more relieved or disappointed when she didn't see him.

They crossed Main and walked along Fifth Street. "Are all the houses here so pretty? I never saw anything like them in Kansas," Deborah said.

Nancy followed her gaze to a neat little Victorian home, white with a bay window and green trim. Nancy shook her head. "Not all of the houses are pretty. Across town, there are some awfully shabby shacks. But most of the town is like this."

"Someday, when I have some time off, I'm going to walk around and see the town."

"You should have someone go with you. I bet there are any number of gentlemen who would be happy to show you around. Some of Tom's friends are single, and most are very nice."

Deborah frowned as she looked down at the shorter woman. She wanted it quickly understood that she was not in the market for a man. She did not think her wounded heart would welcome the possibility of being broken again if a smaller, prettier woman came along.

"I've already had one offer from one of my aunt's boarders. But I'm in no hurry to meet men."

Nancy's brows rose, and Deborah gave an inward groan. It was obvious that her denial had come out as a challenge. She would have to be on her guard against Nancy's well-intentioned matchmaking.

"Tomorrow's Sunday. If you have some time tomorrow afternoon, between making lunch and supper, I could come by for you and we could walk around. Tom could watch little Kathleen while she takes a nap."

"I'd like that."

They parted as Nancy turned the corner for home. Deborah continued to the boardinghouse alone. She looked forward to seeing Nancy again. It would be nice to have a woman to talk to who was near her own age. Isolated on the farm, she hadn't had such a friend in years.

She deposited the meat in the icebox and went upstairs to find her aunt. Carrie was busy sweeping out the rooms. "You can go to the linen closet and get fresh towels," she told Deborah.

Deborah looked down the quiet hall. "Is everyone gone?"

Carrie nodded. "Most are at work. Everybody 'cept Old Joe. He hardly ever leaves the house. I have to lure him out to the porch with a slice of pie so I can clean his room. It makes him nervous as a cat to have me in here. I never had a boarder so protective of his belongings. And the poor old man don't have anything, really."

"He's a strange one. I wonder if he's speaking to me again."

Carrie shook her head. "It's hard to know what goes through his mind."

Deborah found the closet and set about putting out the fresh towels. She was curious about Oscar's room. Would he be neat as a pin or messy?

She found her answer as she walked in to set the towels on his night table. The floor was awash in crumpled paper that spilled from an overfilled waste basket. A desk by the window was the source of the ink-splotched work that had been rejected and discarded into the overfilled bin.

She began to gather the papers into a pile to be burned with the trash. Curiosity got the better of her, and she smoothed one of the rumpled sheets. It was an editorial imploring the good citizens to be responsible with their pets. It seemed one resident had let his dog get into his neighbor's chicken coop. The damage had been profound, and the man had been taken to court when he refused to pay.

Deborah wadded it back into a ball. She smoothed out

another and sucked in a sharp breath as she saw her name. It was written over and over at the top of the page. What followed made her gasp. It was a love poem, much too sentimental for her taste. It wandered along, comparing her eyes to jewels and her lips to sweet red apples. And though the beginning was harmless enough, when she recognized the rest of her attributes as borrowed from the Song of Solomon, she felt her cheeks begin to flame.

She felt sure she was the Deborah who had inspired this effort, though she would have thought it more appropriately directed to one of the saloon ladies of Second Street. How dare he write such intimate verse?

She rose, clutching it in her hand, intending to take it straight to her aunt to prove that she had been right to discourage him. Then she had another thought. It had not been her right to go through the work that he had discarded. She had invaded his privacy. She could hardly go to him and complain. Nor could she go to her aunt, who would likely tell her that she'd been wrong to go through a tenant's trash and then complain about the contents. And it was true. She'd had no right to do it.

She would have to keep her mouth shut. But she didn't have to forget what she'd read. And she didn't intend to show more than the barest civility to the poem's author.

She managed to avoid Oscar until after supper that evening. When she finished washing the last supper plate, Carrie asked her to carry their extra eggs to another boardinghouse to trade for butter.

Deborah packed them in a basket and set off alone to follow Carrie's directions through town. She heard someone call her name, and she groaned. She kept walking, pretending not to hear. Yet, Oscar caught up with her before she reached the end of the block. He jostled against her elbow and smiled up at her. His scrawny handlebar mustache twitched nervously.

"I know your aunt doesn't approve of you keeping company with the tenants, but I've been waiting for a chance to speak to you alone."

"You're right. Carrie doesn't approve. So you'd better tell me what's on your mind and then be on your way."

A shiver crept down her spine. He must have been watching for her ever since supper and had seen her leave the house. She felt terribly awkward in his company now that she'd found the letter. And she couldn't even tell him why.

He rubbed his jaw, pulling the skin tight across his lean face. "Couldn't we go somewhere and sit for a bit? I could buy you a cup of coffee."

She shook her head. "I'm on an errand for my aunt. In fact, I think we should keep walking."

He scurried to keep up with her.

Finally, he took her elbow so that he could stay in step. "Do you know you're the most beautiful creature I've ever seen? I dreamed about you last night. There must be some way to convince your aunt to give me a chance to court you."

Deborah avoided looking at him. "I'm afraid there's no chance. She feels strongly about her rules."

"Surely there are no rules to keep me from walking you about town. At least then I can talk to you."

Deborah was stumped on that one. How, indeed, could she keep him from following her about?

"Carrie might not like it if she found out," she said lamely.

"Then you can blame it all on me. She won't want to lose a tenant."

"I suppose not."

They reached a corner and he tugged her to a halt, saying, "I worked nearly all night to come up with a way to tell you how I feel about you. I've written you a poem."

He pulled a folded paper from his coat pocket and shoved it toward Deborah, who froze, staring at the paper as though it might bite.

She licked her dry lips and said, "It was kind of you, but we really don't know each other well enough for a poem."

"I feel I've known you all my life."

He forced the letter into her hand, and she began to feel irritated.

When she didn't open it, he said, "Read it. I want you to know how I feel."

Deborah felt her cheeks heat as she debated what to do. Finally, under his expectant scrutiny, she unfolded the paper and scanned the lines. To her relief, he had removed some of the more intimate passages, leaving a syrupy tribute to her virtues.

She shoved the letter into the pocket of her skirt. "This was flattering, but if you knew me better, you'd know it's not at all true."

"I'd give a lot for the chance to decide that for myself."

She began walking again, feeling desperate to rid herself of his persistent adoration. The last thing she wanted was a man who would put her on a pedestal, forcing her sense of worth to plummet every time she failed to live up to what he expected.

In her agitation, she failed to watch where she was going

as she rounded a sharp corner. The next thing she knew, she'd run headlong into what felt like a brick wall. Yet as the sharp edge of a badge poked into her shoulder, she realized that the muscular chest of Sheriff Taylor had stopped her in her tracks.

Chapter Three

Deborah gasped as Jake clasped her arms to steady her. Then he held her in front of him to stare into her face. A bemused smile curved his lips.

"Why, Miss Palmer, I might have known it was you. You seem to have a habit of walking without looking."

Deborah clamped her teeth, holding back a sharp retort. When she'd gathered her self-control she said, "I was distracted by my companion."

Jake released her, and she felt a tingling warmth where his hands had rested. His gaze flicked over Oscar. "I can see why you were utterly absorbed, if Oscar talks as dramatically as he writes."

Deborah didn't miss the sarcasm in his tone. Neither did Oscar, who retorted, "Some of us believe it's important to warn people of danger. It helps them get prepared."

"Inventing a phony report of smallpox didn't help. It created a panic."

Oscar glared up at the big man. "That's a false accusation. I honestly believed there was danger."

33

Jake looked skeptical. "You believed it would sell papers."

Oscar scowled. "I'm not going to argue with you, Sheriff. I could easily believe you'd abuse your power and haul me to jail."

"You'd love that, wouldn't you?"

Deborah began to worry that Oscar would provoke Jake into doing something he'd regret. Making a quick decision, she stepped in.

"This is very insightful gentlemen, but I'm on an errand, so if you'll excuse me—"

She knew if she started on her way, Oscar would scurry along to catch up.

To her surprise, it was Jake who acted first. "Not so fast, Miss Palmer. I'm afraid I have a matter of a minor violation to discuss with you."

He turned to Oscar. "I'll walk Miss Palmer wherever she's going."

He steered her forward.

Deborah frowned. "If it's about that coach incident, I don't see how I broke the law."

Oscar face went scarlet with fury. "See here, I'll not let you bully her."

Jake leaned down and whispered to Deborah, "I got the impression you'd like to be rid of him. If I was wrong, just say the word and I'll leave you two alone."

Deborah was surprised by his insight. She couldn't restrain her grin. "You were right. I'll be forever in your debt if you rescue me."

Jake turned to Oscar and said, "I'm not bullying anybody. I just want to talk to her. You don't mind, do you, Miss Palmer?"

"No, it really is all right. I'll see you tomorrow, Oscar."

Since the damsel did not want his assistance, all Oscar could do was stand and scowl as they walked away. Deborah remembered the poem in her pocket and knew he would not easily forgive Jake for coming between them.

Jake smiled at her. His eyes were alight with mischief. It was obvious that he had enjoyed getting one up on Oscar. "You don't like him, do you?" she asked.

"No. He's out to make a name for himself, and he doesn't care who he hurts. He reminds me of a weasel, sniffing around for news."

Deborah laughed. Oscar reminded her of a weasel too. "He can be very persistent. He's taken a liking to me, and I can't seem to get rid of him."

Jake tipped his hat to her. "I'm glad I came by when I did. It was a pleasure to be at your service. And now that you owe me a debt, I've thought of a way you can pay me back."

Deborah raised her brows, wondering what he would say. Jake had a way of arousing her curiosity. Something about his cool reserve challenged her, like an unsolved riddle.

"And how can I pay you back?"

"Come and have ice cream with me."

He watched her closely, trying to guess what she would say. They knew little about each other. And while he didn't want to press her, he also didn't want to miss an opportunity to get to know her better.

He was relieved to see her eyes light up. "I love ice cream. I had it only once before, when I was a little girl. I remember it as the most wonderful thing I ever tasted."

Jake smiled at her enthusiasm. "It's not hard to come by.

You can buy it here all year. And it sure tastes good on a hot summer day."

Deborah smiled. "It sounds like you've had enough to be an expert." She paused to read a sign. "Here's the house I'm looking for. I have to deliver my aunt's eggs. She's trading them for butter."

"Really?" Jake raised a brow. "Mrs. Nealy owns this place. She was a good friend to my mother. I'll come in with you."

He walked in with her and introduced her to the woman who owned the boardinghouse. She was plump and friendly but so busy pressing church clothes with her flat iron that she paused to visit for only a few minutes, after she traded Deborah butter for the eggs.

They left Mrs. Nealy to her work and walked out onto the street. Jake led the way to the tiny ice cream shop nestled in the downstairs parlor of a handsome redbrick hotel. They settled at a tiny table that seemed too small to accommodate either set of their long legs.

Deborah was aware of the stares of the other patrons and was glad to be sitting back in a corner. She wondered if there would be gossip about the sheriff and the new girl in town.

"They have two flavors to choose from. But come summer, they'll have strawberry too," Jake said.

Deborah chose vanilla; Jake chose chocolate.

Her eyes widened in anticipation when it arrived, two generous scoops in a delicate cut-glass bowl. She took a bite and savored the vanilla fragrance and the delightful smoothness as it spread over her tongue. She closed her eyes and tasted the lingering sweetness.

She opened her eyes to see Jake watching her. "Is it as good as you remembered?"

"Better. In fact, I'm enjoying it so much, it should add to my debt."

He grinned as he watched her relish another spoonful. "Then I guess I get another chance. Let's say you owe me until we find something you don't like."

She tilted her head and said dryly, "That might take a while. I grew up on a farm and we didn't have a lot of amusement."

"Then you might owe me for some time, especially if I rescue you from Oscar again."

"I don't mind owing you for that."

Though they ate in silence for a bit, Jake was keenly aware of every move she made—and of his growing admiration for her. Deborah didn't try to feign sophistication like some women he knew. She wasn't afraid to admit she was a farm girl, or to let him see how much she enjoyed this simple pleasure. Unless he was sorely mistaken, here was a woman who was exactly as she appeared. And he liked that.

Deborah studied him as he quietly indulged in his treat. He had managed so easily to get what Oscar could not— her willing company. And he had done it without falling all over himself and fawning over her. In fact, his cool reserve was a welcome change from Oscar's heavy-handed adoration.

"How long have you been a sheriff?" Deborah asked.

"Six years, ever since I turned twenty-one."

"What did you do before that?"

"A little of everything. I worked at the feed store and

then for the blacksmith to support my ma when she got tuberculosis. She died from it eight years ago."

"I'm sorry. You must miss her."

He nodded. "She was a good woman. She took care of me by herself when Pa left. She was never strong after that, and the hard work didn't help."

The talk about his pa made Deborah wistful. "Do you remember your pa?"

"Barely. He up and left for good when I was still a boy. Before that, he hardly took care of us. He was always out looking for silver or gold, hoping to find the next big lode. Ma thought he might have found some and taken off for California. He talked about going there. But as far as I know, he never found enough to pay for a trip."

"My father came here when I was a child. He staked out a claim. And then he disappeared. We never saw him again. Ma believes he ran off, but I'm sure he didn't. He always meant to come back to us."

"What stopped him?" Jake asked.

"I don't know. He had a partner, and I think his partner—"

She stared aghast at Jake. A sudden and awful realization swept over her. Her face paled as she suddenly remembered where she'd heard the name Taylor. "Pa's partner's name was Taylor. Could your father have been his partner?"

Jake felt uneasy. "Probably. There are no other Taylors in town that I know of."

She stood up so quickly she nearly knocked over her chair. "The murdering scoundrel ran off with the silver after he killed my father."

Jake stared at her. A puzzled frown creased his brow. "What are you talking about?"

Her dark eyes flashed as she glared down at him. Every eye in the place was on them. "My father loved his family. He never would have left us. He didn't come home because he couldn't. My aunt believes it and so do I. He was murdered."

Jake had been a man of the law for long enough to know that evidence was required before a conviction. For the life of him, he didn't see where Deborah found any proof of a murder. Before he could object, she grabbed the package of butter and said, "Thank you for the ice cream."

She spun away and added, "I don't think I should be keeping company with you."

He stared at her retreating figure, shoulders squared on her tall frame as she stalked out the door. Even though she was angry, she managed a dignified departure.

Surprise had glued him to his seat. Now, as it dissolved, he shoved back his chair and got to his feet. The room was quiet. No doubt each patron had heard every word. Yet no one met his eyes as he passed through the room. They were embarrassed for him, he thought. He clamped his jaw. Thanks to this outlandish accusation, he'd have to find a way to clear his family's name.

He stared down the street and saw Deborah striding away at a quick pace. She might have long legs, but his were even longer. He set off behind her, catching up with her just after she turned the corner to the boardinghouse. He grasped her elbow and said, "Whoa, there. Since you were so hasty, I'd like to have my say."

She tugged at his grip, but he held tightly to her arm.

Her dark eyes flashed. "Do I have a choice, or will you arrest me if I don't listen?"

"Don't be ridiculous. I'm just asking for a little courtesy."

He was keenly aware of curious looks from passersby but far too irate to care.

Deborah felt her heart ramming into her ribs and admitted to herself that he looked intimidating, squinting down at her with narrowed eyes, his mouth pressed into a hard line.

He pulled her over to the lawn of a little cottage where they stood under a towering pine. "Let's talk over here, where we're not in the path."

She freed her arm from his grasp. "You can let go of me. I'm not going to run away."

He dropped his hands to his sides. His clenched fingers attested to his frustration. "You made an accusation, and I'd like to hear the evidence. I want to see proof of the murder."

Deborah let out a long breath. "I don't have proof. But your father was the last person to see my father alive."

"That simple fact doesn't prove a case of murder. For all I know, your father might have killed my pa."

Deborah's eyes widened with shock. "If that's a joke, it's not funny. My father would never do something like that."

He reached toward her to prevent her from making an angry escape. But she stood her ground, daring him to refute her statement, for there was no doubt in her mind that a Taylor had murdered a Palmer.

He rubbed his chin and said, "I don't think my pa would have murdered anybody. I'll admit he was a no-account drunkard who didn't take care of his family. He would have let us starve if Ma hadn't taken in laundry and baked pies and cakes for the hotels. He had a hot temper and could be rough on his mules, but I never saw him start a fight, and he never beat us."

Deborah considered his words. "Then what do you think happened?"

"I don't know. I never thought about how odd it was, both of them disappearing at the same time. I think I'll check public records to see if they were really partners. It'll be recorded there if they were. Then we can see what else we can learn."

Deborah felt a surge of excitement. The man that she'd decided was her enemy only a few moments before was offering to help her discover what had happened to Pa. What would it be like to finally know? After all the long years of wondering, would she be able to accept the answer?

No matter what pain it might cause, she knew the truth was better than the black void that had haunted her all these years. And with the aid of a sheriff, she might stand a chance of getting to that truth. She'd been hasty and unfair in blaming Jake for the actions of his father. Though she still felt confident that the elder Taylor was the murderer, Jake could have had no knowledge or part in it if he was willing to open a search.

She took a deep steady breath and said, "I was wrong to get so worked up. And you're right. I don't have any evidence. I'd welcome your help."

"Then it's settled that we have a truce unless you find there's a good reason to hate me?"

Deborah managed a weak smile. "That's fair enough."

"I'll look at the records on Monday and let you know what I find. Then maybe we can nose around their claim and see what we uncover there. I listened to my ma when she said he up and ran off. Now you've made me wonder."

"My ma always said the same thing. But I've never believed it."

"Maybe we'll prove them wrong."

She looked into his eyes. The indignation had been replaced by warmth so keen that it touched her very core. She had a notion that Jake Taylor did not easily express his deepest feelings. Those she would find veiled yet open for reading if only she looked deeply into his eyes.

He offered his arm. "May I walk you home?"

She accepted without hesitation. "I'd like that."

He walked her to the boardinghouse. Old Joe sat rocking on the porch. He eyed them warily.

"Hi, Joe," Deborah greeted. "Maybe you could answer a question for us."

Joe kept rocking.

Jake stuck his foot under the chair to stop its motion.

Joe looked up at them.

"You remember my father, Roy Taylor, don't you, Joe?"

Joe nodded. He could hardly pretend not to hear Jake's booming voice.

"Was he a partner with my father, Ed Palmer?" Deborah rushed to ask.

Joe's bushy white brows drew together in a frown. "I don't 'member much about those days. I s'pose they could have been partners. It was a long time ago."

"Do you know what happened to them?" Deborah persisted.

Joe stared down at the porch. "Most folks think they left town."

Deborah sighed, feeling a stab of disappointment. Here was a man who'd known both fathers. Yet, it was obvious they'd get no useful information from Joe.

Jake removed his foot and the old man resumed his rocking.

Deborah turned to Jake. "It would have been helpful if he could have told us something."

"Guess his memory is not what it used to be. I'll check on those records and let you know what I find out."

She smiled up at him. Amber flecks showed in her eyes. She looked womanly: soft and sun-warmed.

"I'd better get this butter inside before Carrie sends Pete out to look for me."

She flashed him a smile before she turned to go in. "Thank you for your help, Sheriff, and for the ice cream treat."

He tipped his hat. "My pleasure. Have a good evening."

After Deborah entered the house, she eased the screen door shut and watched Jake walk down the sidewalk. He was a fine figure of a man. So tall and lean. His broad shoulders stretched the fabric of his coat.

And yet, she'd seen that he was a tolerant man also. Hadn't he come after her and offered his help after she'd stormed away? Many men would have held a grudge after having their father accused of murder.

She found herself comparing Jake to Timothy, her beau from home. Timothy had been a good man, a solid worker. But had he truly cared for her? When she stood on the porch with Jake, she'd imagined he wanted to kiss her. She'd taken buggy rides with Timothy for the last two years, and he'd never tried to kiss her. He'd talked a lot about his plans for his farm. Yet he'd never leaned toward her, listening carefully to what she had to say, as Jake had done in the ice cream parlor.

She shivered. It seemed obvious now that Timothy had never loved her. He'd never found her attractive. They were friends and, as it had seemed their destiny to marry, he'd accepted his fate. But she could never have felt beautiful with Timothy—only big and clumsy like an ox. For the first time, Deborah was glad that a new girl had come into his life.

Carrie's voice startled her from her reverie.

"Now I see what holds you glued to the door. That wouldn't be Sheriff Taylor walking you home, would it?"

Deborah felt her face flush. She was sure her eyes held pure guilt as she turned to face her aunt.

"We stopped off for ice cream. I hope you don't mind. I have the butter right here."

"Mind? Of course I don't mind. But it explains a thing or two. Oscar came barreling into the house 'bout an hour ago, madder than a hornet. Did he see you go off with the sheriff?"

"He did. Jake rescued me from him when he followed me to get your butter." Deborah couldn't help the grin that slid across her face.

Carrie laughed. "Little ol' Oscar was fit to be tied. His face was purple as a prune when he went up those stairs."

"I'm sorry he was mad. He seems to be determined to force his attentions on me. Maybe this will be the end of it."

"I wouldn't count on it. It was the sheriff he was muttering about, not you."

Deborah was glad not to see Oscar when she made her

way to her room after pressing some clothes and setting out the fixings for Sunday breakfast. She settled down with *Pilgrim's Progress* and forgot all about the men in her life.

The next morning, she rose early to help with breakfast. Pete came into the kitchen from doing his chores and from a quick walk to buy a paper. He handed it to Deborah. "Something in here I think you might want to see."

While Carrie peered over her shoulder, Deborah read an editorial by Oscar Evans blasting the sheriff for abusing his power. He recounted the incident of her rescue from his own point of view. She scanned the lines that began:

Yesterday, in a gross abuse of power, a young woman was forcibly removed from a private conversation with an upstanding citizen when the sheriff decided to detain her in order to compete for her attention. The office of sheriff is a sacred trust and not to be exploited. It should make all good citizens wonder if our women are safe from his perusal. What threat might he have used to secure her cooperation when he escorted away my fair young friend?

It went on, exalting the office of sheriff while denouncing the behavior of the office's current occupant.

Deborah groaned. Surely no one would take these accusations seriously. It was obvious that people respected Jake. And with good reason, no doubt. Yet, the article was sure to cause him embarrassment. And it was all her fault. After all, he had been acting on her behalf.

When she served breakfast, it was all she could do to keep from using her strong farm-girl arm to slap the smirk off Oscar's face. He looked up as she plopped a plate of hotcakes in front of him.

"The sheriff will think twice before forcing his attentions on you again."

She scowled as she paused in serving the others to say, "The sheriff and I were already friends. As a matter of fact, I enjoyed his company. After breakfast, I expect you to march straight upstairs and write a retraction for tomorrow's paper."

Oscar puffed out his scrawny chest. "I'll do no such thing. He's got away with bullying this town long enough. He thinks he can do whatever he likes."

She set down the other plates. Every tenant had eyes glued to her face.

"If you have a personal grudge against the sheriff, that's your business. But I won't have you using me to turn people against him."

"It's not a grudge. It's keen observation."

"Then observe someone besides me. I'm not speaking to you again until you take back what you said."

She stormed from the dining room to fetch the plate of sausages that Carrie had ready to serve. One look at the angry flush on her face made Carrie ask, "Whatever got into you?"

"Oscar. I told him I'm not speaking to him until he retracts what he wrote about Jake."

Carrie hesitated before she handed her the plate. "I know you like Jake and I do too. But this is between you and Oscar to work out. Don't be upsetting my other boarders with a lot of angry talk."

Deborah's indignation was tinged with chagrin. "I'm sorry. I didn't think about that."

Carrie handed her the plate. "That's all right. It'll give them something to talk about for a while."

She served with a smile, yet ignored Oscar's attempts to persuade her to his point of view. He lingered as she cleared the table. "I'm not the only one who had something to say about this. The other paper had a report about that argument between the two of you. Why don't you check that out before you get so mad at me?"

Deborah groaned. She wondered what the other paper had said. And she wondered if Jake would be able to hold up his head in this town now that she'd come.

After they'd cleaned up the kitchen, Deborah walked to the corner to buy a paper from the young boy who was selling them. Deborah paid him and began looking for the article by Oscar's competitor.

She glanced around her before looking for the article. A few people were strolling about. Was it her imagination, or was she receiving more than her share of sly glances?

She decided to take the paper home and read the story from the privacy of her room. Then she would decide whether to venture out to church.

She covered the ground in long strides, a single purpose in mind. The sooner she reached her room, the sooner she would know what had been said about them.

She slipped in through the kitchen door and scurried up to her room. After she'd closed the door behind her, she sank onto her bed and riffled through the pages until she found the story.

She scanned the lines and moaned. She'd thought nothing could be more upsetting than Oscar's article condemning Jake. But she'd been wrong.

Chapter Four

The story glared prominently from the second page of the paper. With bold presumption, the author reported that the sheriff had set his hat for the new gal in town. While it didn't mention her by name, it mentioned that she was Carrie's niece and that she was as hot tempered as a firecracker. The author advised the sheriff to stay on his toes if he hoped to keep her happy.

She ground her teeth at the ribbing it gave Jake, saying as how she'd dressed him down good and proper and cut a big man down to size. It went on with tongue-in-cheek jocularity, poking fun at the both of them. She wished she knew who'd written the story so she could tell him just what she thought of it. Then again, she'd likely only end up as the subject of another story.

She was sure Jake had seen the papers by now. She wondered if he was terribly upset. Their friendship had seemed secure when they parted last night. Now she wondered if he'd ever want to see her again. She wished she could go back and wipe out what she'd said. It was so unlike her to lose her temper like that. But she had been shocked by the realization that she might be sitting face-to-face with the son of her father's killer. And because she was beginning to like Jake, her disloyalty had shocked her to her toes.

She pulled her legs onto the bed and settled herself against the heavy iron headboard. She intended to stay here all morning, cowering in her room. The less she saw of the outside world, the happier she'd be.

She was still brooding when Carrie knocked on the door. Deborah looked at the clock. It wasn't time yet to help with Sunday dinner, so she wondered what Carrie could want.

"Deborah, you in there? You have a visitor."

Deborah sighed. She was willing to bet it was yet another reporter who wanted to get the real story about the newly arrived shrew. Well, he was in for a big disappointment, because she wasn't going to give it to him.

She opened the door. "Who is it?"

She intended to tell Carrie that she wasn't coming down.

"It's Jake. He wants to talk to you."

Deborah felt her heart lurch. She didn't feel ready to see him. She didn't feel ready to see anyone after the fine first impression she'd made on this town. But she couldn't hide like a coward from Jake when it was her fault they were in this mess. So she might as well resign herself to facing his justifiable irritation.

"Tell him I'll be right down."

She stopped off to wash her face and tidy her hair. When she couldn't think of anything else to delay her, she padded down the stairs. He was waiting for her in the parlor, passing the time with Pete. She blushed as the men looked up.

She noticed that Jake was decked out in dark woolen

trousers. A fresh white shirt peeked from beneath his coat.

"I've come to escort you to church if you have a mind to go," Jake said.

Deborah swallowed uneasily. "I wasn't planning on going. I thought it might be awkward after what was in the papers."

Jake studied her a moment, then asked, "Will you come out to the porch, where we can have a talk?"

Deborah nodded and followed him out the screen door and onto the porch. Jake turned to face her. "You're not letting those stories upset you, are you?"

She stared, dumbfounded. "Aren't you?"

"Of course not. This isn't the first time I've been the center of some half-baked story. If I worried about every one of them, I'd be miserable. Besides, it'll blow over. You'll see."

She blinked at him. "I thought you'd be furious with me."

He shook his head. "Oscar's always looking for a way to get back at me. If it hadn't been this story, it would have been another. Anyway, you couldn't have known you'd land us in the paper."

He ginned at her. "Pete told me you lectured Oscar in the dining room, wanting him to retract the story. I'm grateful for that, though I bet Oscar's surprised you weren't glad to see me put in my place."

"That's true." She smiled, for the first time seeing a thread of humor in the situation.

"Come with me to church," he urged.

Deborah hesitated. "Won't it fuel the gossip if folks see us together?"

"It's the best thing that could happen. Everybody will

see that I get along perfectly well with a mild-mannered and well-bred lady."

Deborah grinned. "Now you're flattering me. Though I can't help but admit it feels good after having my heart broken and rejected. I'll get my hat and be right back."

She hummed as she skimmed up the stairs, returning with her only decent hat pressed upon her head. The cream fabric was worn, and the tiny red silk roses on the side were faded, but it had a nice wide brim and would serve to keep the high mountain sun off her face.

Carrie glanced up from the mending she was doing in the parlor. "You going out?"

"Jake asked me to church, and I decided to go."

"I thought you would." Carrie's lips twitched, resisting a smile as Jake offered Deborah his arm and they set off together.

Though she wore a long-sleeved gingham dress printed with tiny violets, the touch of early coolness remained, raising goose bumps along her arms. She stared into a cloudless sky and guessed that by the time they left church the sun would have stirred itself to bake down on the town. Then, by late afternoon, it would hide its warmth again and send a chill into the air.

Jake led her to the small-frame building of the Methodist Episcopal Church on Fourth Street. She blushed at the openly curious glances of the congregation. Yet, when several women went out of their way to welcome her, the greetings seemed so sincere that she began to relax.

The singing and the preaching brought back nostalgic memories of her childhood in Kansas. Ma had seen that they were scrubbed and seated in their family pew each week. While her brothers had squirmed, Deborah had patiently awaited the opportunity to meet up with Timothy in the churchyard after service.

She remembered the anticipation she'd felt when there was to be a box lunch and Timothy was to sit with her. She bit her lip and forced the memory aside. It was a girlhood dream that had outlived its time. She was a woman now, and she was sure that the man sitting beside her could make her forget all about Timothy—if he had a mind to try.

When church ended and they filed out, Deborah received greetings and friendly interest from women with husbands and children in tow. The unattached young women gave her cool looks and no greetings at all.

She allowed Jake to take her arm, realizing that this tall blond Viking was husband bait for the single women in town. She'd make few friends by parading around town holding his arm. And yet, it felt good to be the one chosen, instead of the one discarded, this time.

The sun warmed their shoulders as they strolled back to the boardinghouse. The scent of lilac mixed with the earthy smell of horses as the town stirred to life.

Jake looked down at Deborah, admiring her profile of creamy sculpted cheek, long dark lashes, and a slightly tipped-up nose. A gentle breeze ruffled feathery chestnut hair that fell softly onto her shoulders. How could any man be fool enough not to recognize the beauty of this tall, long-legged filly? Her old beau must have been blind to reject Deborah for another gal.

He decided to push his luck. "I'm sure you have to help with Sunday dinner, but afterward, would you like to take a walk around town?"

She smiled up at him. "I'd love to, but I promised Nancy Parker a visit this afternoon."

Jake stifled his disappointment and said, "Maybe another time."

"Sure. I'd love to see more of Ouray."

"You'd love the waterfall where Canyon Creek drops down into the gorge at Box Canyon. And I could show you some hot springs."

"Hot springs?"

"Mineral pools. The Indians used them for medical purposes. They're supposed to have healing properties. I don't know about that, but that warm water feels real good."

Deborah nodded. "My feet could use a soak after a long day working with Carrie."

"She pretty demanding?"

"She's fair and easier to please than my ma. Still, I can see why her boardinghouse has a reputation for being clean."

"Next Sunday, let's go and see the falls. Then we'll stop and soak your aching feet."

Deborah laughed. "You've got a deal. I won't make any other plans."

They parted at the boardinghouse, and Deborah hustled in to change her dress and help fry chicken and mash a huge pot of potatoes. They boiled collard greens and sliced a loaf of fresh bread. Then Deborah set all the food out on the table.

Oscar cast her a nervous glance and asked, "Did you have a nice morning?"

"It was very pleasant, thank you."

He let out his breath, obviously relieved that she was speaking to him in spite of her threat.

For her part, Deborah decided that if Jake was willing to let it all blow over, she would do the same. She only hoped that Oscar didn't take her forgiveness to be the result of his irresistible charm.

He caught her wrist as she reached to clear the plates after they'd finished their meal. She sighed impatiently, feeling hungry and ready to eat her own dinner.

"Come walk with me this afternoon."

"I can't. I've promised my friend Nancy I'll go see her."

He thought a moment and said, "There's a concert at the opera house on Friday night. We could go to that."

"I don't want to go to a concert on Friday. So, if you'll let go of my hand, I've got work to do."

He released her and pulled his brows into a pouting frown. "What do you like to do?"

She resisted the urge to tell him there was nothing that would entice her into spending time with him. Instead she reminded him, "I'm not supposed to keep company with the boarders. My aunt's rule, remember?"

Oscar rose from the table and shot back over his shoulder, "Then tell your aunt that I just might have to find myself another place to live."

Deborah cleared the table before sinking into a chair at the kitchen table. Carrie and Pete had already begun their lunch. She wondered how Carrie would take the news that Deborah might have lost them a tenant.

"What's wrong with you? You look like you lost your best friend," Carried said.

"That couldn't be further from the truth."

Deborah told them how Oscar had threatened to find anther place to live.

Pete leaned forward and said, "Do you think we'd go

bankrupt if the little weasel left us? Let him go, I say. I can hardly stand the sight of him after what he said about the sheriff."

Carrie burst out laughing. "Why, Pete Turner, I've never heard you talk that way about a boarder before. Anyway, if he moves out, Deborah will lose her excuse not to keep company with him."

"I should have told him from the start that I think he's obnoxious," Deborah said.

"I think your problem will solve itself if you keep seeing the sheriff. Even Oscar should get that message," Carrie said.

"I barely know the sheriff. We're friends and no more," Deborah protested. She had no intention of letting anyone, including herself, jump to conclusions about Jake's intentions toward her. She'd been jilted once and endured the humiliation that had driven her from home. She had no desire to do it again.

Carrie studied her niece. "I've known Jake since he was a little boy. And it's plain he likes you. He's not the sort to go chasing after women, though I've seen a few go chasing after him."

Deborah felt both pleased and embarrassed. She decided to change the course of the conversation. "Did you know Jake's father was Pa's partner?"

"I knew it," said Pete. "Jake's nothing like his pa, though. That old man was drunk more than he was sober. He left his poor wife to fend for herself and the young 'un. She was always a sickly sort, pale and thin. As soon as Jake got big enough, he busied himself getting jobs so she wouldn't have to work so hard. It was too late by then. The poor thing died a few years after her no-good husband disappeared."

"Jake doesn't think his pa killed mine. He's going to

check and see if they both registered their claim on the mine. Then we're going to do a little digging around to see if we can find any clues to prove what really happened."

Carrie shook her head. "I know Jake doesn't want to face it, but I think it's pretty obvious what happened. His pa killed yours and then hightailed it out of town. He probably lived high on the silver they found until it ran out. Of course he couldn't come back after that."

In her heart, Deborah believed her aunt was right. And she would prove it. She would prove that Pa had not deserted them but had been taken from them by death. Would knowing this truth soften the tight lines around Ma's mouth or erase the bitterness in her eyes? Deborah hoped so. The family had lived under the dark cloud of abandonment far too long. And if she had it in her power to clear Pa's name, she intended to do it.

She wouldn't do any more accusing in front of Jake, however, until she had some real evidence. She had no desire to antagonize him while he was her partner in solving the mystery.

When the kitchen was put straight, she went to the porch to wait for Nancy to collect her for their walk. Old Joe and Pete were busy with a game of checkers. Deborah paused to study the board. Her scrutiny didn't bother Pete. Yet, she noticed that the longer she watched, the more Joe's hand shook when he reached to move his piece.

She saw Nancy hurrying down the block and walked down to meet her, still wondering just what about her made Joe so nervous.

Nancy took her arm as though they'd known each other for years instead of only three days. "Won't this be fun? I told Tom that I'd be gone at least an hour and not to expect me any sooner."

Deborah laughed. "You sound like you need a break."

"I do. I love being a mother, and I love Kathleen. But she's started to walk and I have to watch her all the time to make sure she doesn't get into trouble."

"I remember when my little sister was small. I used to carry her all around to keep her out of mischief."

"Do you miss your family very much?"

"Not too badly. It's been exciting coming here."

Nancy cast her a curious glance. "I saw the paper this morning. It seems you had a run-in with our sheriff."

Deborah bit her lip, willing the color not to rise in her cheeks. "The reporter misunderstood. We were discussing the fact that our fathers were mining partners. Jake is going to help me find out what happened to my father. Pa came here years ago and never returned."

Nancy frowned. "Oh, Deborah, I'm so sorry. I hope you can find out where he is. Do you think he's still alive?"

Deborah shook her head. "I doubt it. Pa loved us. I could tell. If he could have come home, he would have."

They walked in silence for a while. Deborah felt relieved that the explanation about her father seemed to have distracted Nancy from the story about Deborah and Jake.

They headed up Fifth Street. "Let's walk up Vinegar Hill to Ninth Avenue. I can show you a cabin built on an old mine claim, the Mephistopheles Lode."

"Vinegar Hill?"

Nancy smiled. "Strange name, isn't it? The story has it that in 1875 some men gathered in Judge Long's cabin for Christmas dinner. Since they didn't have any liquor, they fixed up some vinegar and managed to get tipsy. They called the place Vinegar Hill. I bet some of those men had a little trouble getting back down the hill."

"I'd like to see that cabin."

Nancy pointed. "It's right there."

Deborah turned to look. "It doesn't look like much now. Still, I bet they had a great time."

They walked along, headed toward the old mine claim.

"I guess you'll be seeing a lot of Jake if he's helping you find your father."

It seemed that Nancy was not going to be easily distracted from so promising a subject. Deborah would have to be careful to conceal her attraction for the rugged blond man with eyes of periwinkle blue that crinkled at the corners when he smiled. If she let it slip that she liked him, the town would have them engaged to be married before they'd known each other a week.

She realized that Nancy was staring up at her and answered cautiously, "I suppose we'll have to see each other if we're going to solve what happened."

"You say your fathers were partners?"

Deborah nodded.

"Then, since you'll inherit your share of the mine from your mother, that makes you and Jake partners."

Deborah stopped in her tracks to look at Nancy. "I never thought of it like that, though I don't think we'd find much if we started mining. I'm sure Jake's father wouldn't have left the mine if it was still producing silver."

"Is Jake's father still alive?"

"I don't know. They both disappeared and were never heard from again."

Nancy cocked her head. "And no one in town knows what happened to them?"

"No one that I know of. Old Joe knew them, but he doesn't know what became of them."

"That is strange. And how awful for your families. Is that why you came here?"

Deborah hesitated. This was a question she didn't feel like answering just yet. So she decided to hedge. "Not really. It wasn't my idea to start with. You see, my mother sent me to help out my aunt. But now that I'm here, it's like Providence brought me so that I would have a chance to learn the truth. I don't want me and my family to spend the rest of our lives always wondering what happened to Pa. I just hope I can find out."

Nancy patted her arm. "With Jake's help, you'll learn something. Folks around here say he never gives up on anything he sets his mind to. Once, there was a little boy who wandered away in the middle of a blizzard. The rescue party gave up in that awful storm and came back. But Jake didn't give up. He went back out alone and was gone for a day and a night. Everybody thought he'd died in the storm. And then the next afternoon he came trudging back into town holding that little boy. Other than a little frostbite, the child was all right."

Nancy wiped at her eyes. "I feel better living with Tom and my little Kathleen in a town that has Jake for a sheriff. Tom says he's the most stubborn man he's ever known. He's also the best sheriff."

Deborah smiled. "That's good to know. Since my father disappeared such a long time ago, I'll need all the stubborn help I can get to solve what happened."

They reached Ninth Avenue, and Nancy pointed out the old mine claim.

"It must be pretty exciting to go digging and find silver," Nancy said.

"Or disappointing if you don't," Deborah said.

Nancy nodded. "I guess there have been plenty of both disappointment and joy here in Ouray. But a man can get rich with the right find. Look at Camp Bird Mine. Thomas Walsh is getting to be a rich man."

Deborah stared at the old mine cabin and thought that she'd trade any silver she could find for an answer to her puzzle. For only an answer would bring her peace of mind. And that was what she really wanted.

As they walked back, she was seized with an inspiration so urgent that she clasped Nancy's arm and said, "Being rich won't bring Pa back, but it might buy information about what happened to him. What if there is still some silver left in the mine? If I could get to it, I could offer to pay for information about his death. Of course I wouldn't pay unless the person could prove his facts. But isn't it a good idea?"

Nancy stared up doubtfully, her blue eyes wide. "Who would you get to do the mining?"

"I don't know. But there must be someone I could trust."

"Why don't you talk it over with Jake? After all, you're partners."

"That's a wonderful idea. I'll see him tomorrow. I hope he likes the idea."

Nancy looked less than convinced, but she didn't comment.

They parted at Fifth Street, where Deborah promised to keep Nancy up on what she found out. The rest of the way to the boardinghouse, Deborah dreamed of having someone come forward to offer information. All she needed was that reward.

She waited impatiently for Jake all day as she went about her Monday duties. Finally, supper came and went. By seven o'clock, the dishes had been put away and the house tidied for the night. She took her shawl and wandered onto the porch as though she could will him to come walking down the street. She'd nearly given up to go inside when he appeared.

He smiled when he saw her.

She hurried toward him, looking eager for information, and Jake wondered what it would feel like to have a woman like Deborah waiting for him to come home each night. After his mother died, he'd disliked the solitude of coming home to an empty house. Over the years, he'd got used to it and convinced himself that he was fine in his bachelor ways. After all, having a wife who would nag or scold was worse than no wife at all.

Yet, now that he'd met Deborah, he found himself engaging in flights of fancy. Though he'd told himself firmly that it had to stop, it took only one look at her as she glided toward him like a stately dark-haired angel to overturn his self-control.

She met him at the street and walked him back to the porch.

"You look hot. Would you like a glass of lemonade?" she asked.

He shook his head. "Maybe in a little while. I came by to tell you that I checked the official records, and our fathers were partners. So it seems you and I inherit the mine. We won't be trespassing if we go up there to look around."

"Nancy was right. That makes us partners too."

She shivered with a sudden foreboding that any partnership between a Taylor and a Palmer could only end in disaster. She shook off the feeling. After all, she would have to trust him if she hoped to get help in finding silver for that reward.

Carrie pushed open the spring door and stepped onto the porch. "You didn't tell me the sheriff was coming by."

She gave Jake a broad smile. "You should come in and taste some apple pie. Deborah made it and, I have to admit, she's a mighty fine cook."

Jake's face lit with approval. "I won't turn down a piece of good pie."

"Well, come on into the kitchen. I have a pot of coffee still on the stove."

Jake followed them into the kitchen.

Deborah felt her spirits sink with disappointment. She'd hoped to have Jake alone to broach the idea of opening up the mine. She didn't want him influenced by Carrie, who often had strong opinions and wouldn't hesitate to state them.

To her relief, Carrie served Jake pie and coffee and then left them alone, facing each other at the kitchen table. Deborah fingered a fold in her skirt as she watched Jake sample the pie.

A grin spread across his face, showing off the dimple in his chin. "This is one mighty fine pie."

"I'm glad you like it."

She took a deep breath and decided the time had come to ask him to become a part-time miner as well as a sheriff.

Chapter Five

I was thinking . . ." Deborah began.

Jake watched her curiously.

"Somebody in town might know what happened to my pa, and yours too. But maybe they've had no reason to tell."

Jake considered this while he speared another bite of pie. "It's possible, I suppose. You have an idea?"

She leaned forward, eager to convince him. "I do. What if we were to reopen the mine and do some digging? We might find a little silver, enough to offer a reward to anyone who could tell us what happened."

Jake frowned as he considered her idea. "There's no guarantee we'd find silver if we opened the mine. Besides, sulfur in the water causes nails to rust and fall right out, so it wouldn't be safe to go in until we'd done a lot of shoring up."

"But isn't it worth a try? I'm willing to work hard on it myself, but I'd like your help."

As he looked into her hopeful face, he found the arguments dying on his tongue. He didn't have much hope that, for all the work it would take, they'd find enough silver to offer a decent reward. But it was something they could work on together. It would give him a reason to spend time with her.

"All right. We'll go look around and see what's left. Maybe we'll find some clues ourselves without digging for silver. Could you get free for a couple of hours tomorrow afternoon?" he asked.

"It's wash day, but if I start early, I bet Carrie would let me have the afternoon off. And please, could we not tell anyone what we're doing? I don't want anybody hanging around, trying to jump our claim."

Jake grinned. "I'd hate to see them tangle with you, so I promise it will be our secret. I'll drop by about one o'clock. You can be back in time to help with supper."

She gave him a bright smile and he decided the glow in her eyes was worth the hard work they were getting into.

She studied him thoughtfully. "Do you believe in destiny? I have the strongest feeling that we were meant to meet and get to the bottom of this."

Jake wanted to tell her that he didn't know if it was destiny or pure chance that had brought her here. Whichever it was, he was intrigued by her now that she had come. He answered thoughtfully, "If we were meant to meet, then there's a reason. It might be to solve what happened to our fathers."

He finished his pie, and they sat talking. He told Deborah what he knew about mining. It wasn't a lot, because he'd been inside a mine only a handful of times. He'd helped his pa dig on the few occasions the elder Taylor had thought he'd found a vein of silver. Each time had been a disappointment until the mine he'd opened with Deborah's pa.

And Jake wasn't sure how much silver they'd taken out of there. Pa had come home drunk and bragged about their find, but Jake had never known whether to believe it was true. If it was, he never shared it with Jake or his mother.

They drifted into childhood reminiscence. Deborah told him how much her family had changed after her pa went away, never to return. Jake's heart went out to the young girl he imagined. If it were in his power to erase the sadness from her past, he intended to do it.

Just as he promised, Jake dropped by at one o'clock the next afternoon. Deborah had finished cleaning the kitchen and had fresh sheets and towels in all of the rooms. She was rosy-cheeked from all her activity, but her eyes were bright with anticipation.

She pulled a faded bonnet from a rack beside the parlor door and preceded him down the porch steps. It was a warm afternoon, one that would have made her lethargic if not for her excitement about seeing the mine.

Jake held a lantern in one hand. With the other, he took her arm and led her west across Main Street.

"I had to tell Lee where to find me if I was needed, but he won't tell anyone," Jake said, speaking of the man who occasionally served as his deputy.

"Is it far to the mine?"

"Not really. We'll head toward White House Mountain and then walk up Oak Creek Canyon. The claim is in a ravine. It'll take us about a half hour to walk there."

Unlike other women, Deborah's long legs easily kept pace with Jake's stride.

When they reached the ravine, Deborah hiked her skirt up to the top of her boots to negotiate the rocky ground.

She felt lightheaded from the altitude and was tempted to perch on a ledge of flat rock to have a rest. Yet she pushed determinedly on. Surely, she would adapt to the altitude in a day or two. She didn't want Jake to get the idea that she couldn't keep her promise to help him with the work.

Finally he pointed down a dry gulch. She nearly melted with relief when he said, "It's right in here, at the bottom of the cliff."

Deborah followed along, picking her way over the loose stones. At the end of the gulch, she saw a rickety lean-to, its planks weathered by years of neglect. The door hung loose on rusty hinges. The roof, which slanted down from the cliff, had a hole where a rock had rolled down and broken through.

A few yards past the lean-to, she spotted the entrance to the mine. The outer frame was still standing. Two round side beams supported a thick round post that rested below the horizontal cut in the cliff. Deborah judged that she could enter without having to stoop.

She started forward, and Jake reached out to catch her arm. "Not so fast. We can't go charging in there. The supports may be loose. If we bump the wrong board, we could bring a ton of rock down on our heads."

Deborah pulled away, her feelings ruffled. "I was not going to *charge* inside. I was going to look in."

Jake nodded. "Look all you like. But do it from the entrance to the mine."

They peered into the dark recess. A rusty pickax lay propped near the opening. Had Pa used it? Deborah bit her lip to keep it from trembling. This was where he had worked. He had probably swung that very ax that was rusty now with age.

Jake stooped and lit the lantern. He took a step into the mine and held up the lantern for a look around. Deborah followed close at his heels. "I thought you said we'd have to stay outside."

"I'm looking to see what I'll have to do to make it safe to explore this place."

He pointed. "Those nails have come loose from the top boards there, and the side support has fallen in over on the left. I'll have to bring some lumber and nails and shore it up before we can go very far."

Deborah glanced around, looking for any other sign of her father's presence. She shivered. Behind them lay the welcoming sunlight, the sound of birds, and the blue of the sky. She could see only a short way in front of her before the lantern light was swallowed by the abyss.

The mine smelled of damp earth and rotting timber. She felt entombed, and for a moment she was seized by the desire to turn and escape back into the sunshine. Yet her determination held her in place, making her clench her jaw and stand her ground. Now that she was here, nothing was going to keep her from finding out what happened to Pa. She would have to get used to feeling like a mole, because it was going to be dark deep in the mine where they'd begin their search for silver.

Jake shone the lantern across the dirt walls. They were pitted by the shovels and axes that had formed the tunnel. Ahead, a pile of rocks lay scattered across the path, the result of the weakening of an overhead beam.

"I don't see anything here that would tell any stories about our kin. We'll have to wait until we can go farther inside. Let's check the lean-to," Jake suggested.

He nodded for Deborah to precede him. She came blinking into the sunlight and turned to watch him duck to avoid hitting his head on the top beam.

"It's hard to imagine working underground day after day, not even seeing the sun for a week or more," Deborah said.

Jake set down the lantern. "I decided a long time ago it wasn't the life for me."

She walked beside him on the way to the shack. "You like being a sheriff?"

"For now. Someday I'd like to buy me a little ranch up by Ridgeway. Run a few cows."

He pulled open the door, and they stared at the disorder inside. Two moth-eaten cots sat near a rickety potbellied stove. A scattering of pots and pans, long rusted through, sat on the floor, and a dented tin mug lay at Deborah's feet. She reached to pick it up as Jake stared at the battered coffeepot that sat on top of the stove.

He frowned, not liking being haunted by ghosts from his past. He remembered sitting with his pa and drinking from that pot on the few times he'd come here. When they'd finished their beans, Pa had got drunk and fallen asleep, leaving Jake to lie in the dark and feel guilty for leaving Ma home alone. After a few days, he'd always left the mine to go back and care for her.

After Pa disappeared, Jake had visited the lean-to and the mine several times, always fearing he'd find Pa's body. And though he never had, he could never shake the uneasiness that always crept into his bones.

It had been years now since his last return. He thought he'd put thoughts of Pa behind him and moved on with his life. He could have left it that way, if not for a certain young lady. He sighed as he watched Deborah finger the mug, hoping he wouldn't regret his decision to help her. Solving this mystery could bring them both pain. And he didn't want to see another woman he cared about as sad as he'd seen Ma.

She set the mug on the rough wood stool that stood on three wobbly legs. "I guess we won't learn much here either, except that they weren't good at housekeeping."

He met her smile, appreciating her effort to lighten the mood. "Miners don't care much about how they live. They care about the riches they hope to find."

"Well, I guess that makes me a miner, because I hope to find some too. It also reminds me that I'm earning my board by housekeeping. I'd better get back and help Carrie with supper."

They walked slowly back down the ravine.

"I'll come up here in a day or two with that lumber. Once the mine is safe, we can go in and see where they were mining."

Deborah looked up imploringly. "Please don't come without me. I really want to be a part of this."

"When could you come?"

"I have Thursday afternoon off."

"You have my word not to come without you. We'll come again on Thursday if I can get away."

She gave his hard-muscled arm an impulsive squeeze. "You're a thoughtful man, Jake Taylor."

He bent to her upturned face and kissed her lightly on the nose. "And you're a beautiful woman, Deborah Palmer."

Deborah felt her cheeks burn in a furious rush of heat. Still, she kept his arm clasped next to her until they reached the outskirts of town. They parted on Fifth Street, with Jake turning toward his office and Deborah toward the boarding-house.

He tipped his hat. "Until Thursday."

"Until Thursday," she agreed.

She sped lightly along the street, hardly aware of where she was going until she heard someone call her name. She forced herself not to grimace as she saw Oscar waving from an upstairs window of the newspaper office.

"Wait up, Deborah. I'm coming right down."

Deborah considered hurrying away before he could reach her. Yet that would be inexcusably rude. After all, Oscar was a tenant. He paid her aunt good money every month. She owed it to Carrie to be polite to him.

He grinned broadly as he spilled out of the building, so out of breath that she wondered if he'd considered the pos-sibility that she would not wait.

"I have good news for you. There's a concert at the Wright Opera House tonight, and I have two tickets."

"I can't go tonight, Oscar."

"Are you sure? I heard that you want information about your father. I thought I could introduce you around a bit. We could see if anyone knows anything."

She thought it over. It could be a good opportunity. Still, one thing was for sure. Oscar would have to under-stand that, if she agreed, it was only for her father.

"I'll come, Oscar, but only because I want information. Don't think there's anything more."

Oscar threw up his hands. "I only want to help you. That's all."

She doubted his sincerity. And she disliked mixing with

a roomful of strangers. Yet for Pa's sake, she'd do a lot of things she didn't like.

Carrie raised an eyebrow when Deborah told her about her plans. "I did mention to him that you were looking for information about Ed. With him being a reporter, I thought he might be able to help you. I hope you don't mind me telling him."

"I don't mind. I just hope he doesn't get the wrong idea about me agreeing to go with him."

"Knowing Oscar, he'll get the wrong idea. And no matter what you do, there's nothing you can do to stop him."

Deborah sighed. "You're probably right. Let's just hope I'll find out something useful."

She met Oscar downstairs when it was time to walk to the opera house.

He'd dressed carefully in dark pants, suspenders, and a navy shirt under a brown jacket. One look at his slicked-back hair and pleased expression told her he felt he'd succeeded in winning her over.

Deborah secured the pins in her straw hat and pulled her shawl from the hook beside the door. With more than a few doubts as to the wisdom of letting him escort her, she sighed and preceded him out the door.

They reached Main Street and walked past the businesses on the ground floor of the opera house. A small crowd was filing up to the second floor of the ornate building. Oscar greeted a few gentlemen. Deborah couldn't help noticing the lukewarm greetings they returned.

They reached the concert room, where groups of patrons

stood in small knots chatting before the concert began. Oscar led them toward a group of well-dressed men and women. Deborah felt her heart begin to pound. She wasn't used to strangers, and she felt distinctly uncomfortable in this crowd.

Oscar wormed his way into the group and introduced her. "Deborah is hoping that one of you fine citizens might remember her father, Ed Palmer. The last letters he sent came from Ouray, and she's trying to find out what happened to him."

The gentlemen shook their heads, and the ladies professed no memory of him. They returned to their private conversations with a promise to let her know if they thought of anything that would help her.

As they made their way around the room, Deborah found that Oscar made up in boldness whatever he lacked in size. He didn't stop until they had to sit down to hear the lovely young soprano sing ballads to the accompaniment of a piano.

Deborah had a hard time keeping her attention on the performance. She was disappointed to have learned nothing. She glanced at Oscar. He looked to be enjoying himself. He leaned forward in his seat mesmerized by the singer's clear, silky voice.

He turned to Deborah during the intermission and said, "I could listen to this forever. It's romantic, don't you think?"

"It's very pretty, but . . ."

"I know. You came to learn about your father."

They made the rounds of people they had not asked. A few folks remembered Ed but could tell her nothing that would help her follow his trail.

By the time the concert ended, Deborah felt exhausted

and discouraged. She forced a polite smile as they walked down the stairs and out to the street, leaving the beautiful arched windows of the opera house behind.

"I'm sorry we didn't find out more about your father. Did you enjoy the concert?"

"Yes, of course. She sang very nicely. And thank you for introducing me and asking about Pa. I guess the trail is just too cold."

"Don't give up. Someone may remember something. I'll keep digging around a little and see what I can find out."

She smiled down at him. "That's very kind, but I'm sure your job keeps you busy."

"That *is* my job. And solving this mystery would make a great article for the paper. Your aunt tells me that you think his partner murdered him."

Deborah shook her head. The idea of pulling Jake's family into this didn't appeal to her. "I don't know what I think. There are no clues as to what happened."

He gave her arm a squeeze. "You leave it to me. I'm not going to stop until I get to the bottom of this."

They walked the rest of the way home with Oscar talking nonstop about his skill as a reporter and his plans to become the owner of his own newspaper someday. Deborah nodded down at the little man, feeling like an ox walking alongside a mouse. Perhaps it was vain to feel self-conscious about her size. But she couldn't help feeling more at ease when a man like Jake was walking beside her.

"Will you come again to a concert with me?" he asked as they walked to their rooms.

Deborah shook her head. "This was a one-time thing."

His brows puckered in disappointment before he said, "You'll change your mind."

He whistled down the hall to his room while Deborah opened her door, grateful for the solitude of her own quarters.

On Thursday, Jake came for her early in the afternoon. He'd brought a wagon piled with boards, hammers, and nails.

"Now we begin the work," he said as he helped her onto the seat, his large hands spanning easily around her waist.

As they plodded out of town he said, "I heard you went with Oscar to the concert."

She glanced over to see that he didn't look pleased. The idea that he might be jealous gave her a strange sensation of pleasure. Yet, having been brought up to be honest, she said, "I went because there were lots of people there, and he offered to help me ask about my father."

The tense line of Jake's jaw relaxed. "And did you find out anything?"

"No. If anyone knew what happened, I suppose they would have come forward a long time ago."

"Then let's shore up the mine and see if we find anything."

They worked side by side in the dark tunnel while dust and tiny clods of dirt rained down on their heads. Yard by yard, they shored up the mine, replacing rotten beams with strong new ones. Every time they moved the lantern deeper into the tunnel, Deborah looked for signs that her father had been there. Yet all she saw were rusty nails and rotted boards.

By suppertime, they'd shored up the first thirty feet of the mine. Deborah's arms and back ached. She'd bruised her thumb with the hammer and torn her skirt. But she had a good appreciation for the backbreaking work her pa had put into his search for silver.

They stumbled out of the tunnel, and Jake piled the remaining boards near the opening of the mine. "I can come back and work every evening till next Tuesday. We're expecting a shipment of gold, and I've got to be in town, at least till it leaves Ouray."

"Then we'll work until Tuesday. I should be able to get away after supper cleanup each night. We'll have a couple hours of light."

He helped her into the wagon and then grinned broadly at her disheveled appearance. How many women would be both determined and fit enough to go into the bowels of the earth to hold up boards and swing a hammer? Her nose was streaked with mud, and her skirt was bedraggled. Her hair had escaped from the ribbon that had held it back and fell in wisps around her face. She was, by far, the most beautiful woman he had ever seen.

Deborah rubbed self-consciously at her cheek. "I must look an awful sight."

She had been too busy in the mine to think about her appearance. And in the darkness, it didn't seem to matter. Now, in the bright sunlight of late afternoon, she could see the dirt under her nails and the rip in her skirt.

Jake's grin faded to a tender smile. "Has anyone ever told you that you're beautiful? A little dirt can't change that."

He reached out and wiped the smudge off her nose.

Deborah swallowed past the tightness that filled her throat. No one had told her she was beautiful since Pa had gone away. And she'd quickly decided that his opinion was flawed by fatherly love. She was too tall, too big. Yet as she gazed into Jake's admiring eyes, she knew he meant what he said. He really thought she was pretty. And, in spite of the mud, for the first time since she was a child, she *felt* pretty.

She couldn't tear her gaze from his face: the mud streaked across his broad forehead, his firm mouth, his periwinkle eyes. She was as captivated as if she were held hostage. She couldn't move, could hardly breathe.

He leaned toward her and kissed her gently, deepening the kiss as she closed her eyes and leaned into him. He pulled her against him, and she could feel the beat of his heart, the warmth of his skin beneath his shirt. She had never known it could be like this. She'd never thought she could want to stay encircled forever in a man's arms. It had never been like this with Timothy.

When he reluctantly released her, she missed the pressure of his lips, the warmth of his body. The intensity of her emotions confused her. Yet as he ran a finger tenderly along her cheek, she knew she had enjoyed every moment of his kiss.

"I better get you back so you don't miss supper," he said.

Deborah gave a shaky laugh. "I should get cleaned up first. Carrie won't let me in her kitchen looking like this."

Jake shook the reins and started the horses toward town. "Folks will be wondering what we've been up to."

"Then let them wonder. It's no business but our own," she replied saucily.

She kept her stalwart attitude until they pulled in front of the boardinghouse. Oscar was just walking home from work. He paused to stare at them, and Deborah groaned. He was the last person she wanted to see.

While Jake handed her down, Oscar waited at a discreet distance, like a spider ready to pounce. After she told Jake good-bye, she strode toward the porch, with Oscar scurrying along beside her.

"You look awful. What's he done to you?"

"He hasn't *done* anything. We were out poking around outdoors to see if we could find clues about our fathers."

Oscar clasped her elbow before she could escape into the house.

"They were partners. I verified it today. And someone told me Jake got a package a few years ago with things from his father. I believe old Roy sent the stuff. And I bet Jake knows where he is and that they both know what happened to your pa."

Deborah caught her lip between her teeth, stunned by the information.

"You might try asking your sheriff friend to come clean with you about what he knows." Oscar sounded smug.

"I intend to, Oscar. Thank you for the information."

She turned away.

Her thoughts were a jumble of confusion. Why hadn't Jake told her about the package? Was it because he knew where Roy was hiding out? In that case, what else did he know that he wasn't telling her?

She could hardly believe Jake had lied to her. Yet, as she scrubbed herself raw, she knew that while she could easily get rid of the dirt, she could not so easily rid herself of the suspicion that lodged in her mind. For that, she'd need some good explanation.

Chapter Six

Deborah spent a restless night trying to convince herself that Jake would not play her for a fool. He would not let her dig for silver to offer a reward for information about her father if he knew what had happened.

By the time he came to walk her to the mine that evening, she had to fight her instinct to fly at him and demand an explanation. Instead she walked quietly by his side until they reached the street, and then halted, determined not to take another step until she had an explanation.

"I heard yesterday that you got a package from your pa a few years ago. Why didn't you tell me about it?"

Jake stared down at her. A puzzled frown gave way to a nod of recollection. "I'd forgotten about it. It was about three years after he disappeared. I always wondered why he would send his things if he was still alive, and why someone else would send them if he were dead—unless he died a long way from home."

"You never heard from him again?"

Jake shook his head. "I've got the package at the office. We can go over and take a look if you like."

"I'd like that."

They walked over to the jail. Jake's office was in the front room. He rummaged through a drawer in his desk and produced a plain brown package. He dumped the contents on the desk. There wasn't much to see: a tin of tobacco, a pocket watch with a cracked cover, a few interesting rocks . . . another watch.

Why would a man have two watches? She picked it up and fingered it. She turned it to read the initials that were carved on the smooth round back: E.L.P.

With a sudden shock she realized that she'd seen this watch when she was a little girl. Her fingers shook as she held it tightly by the chain.

"This was my father's watch. It has his initials."

Jake studied the watch. "I never looked at it closely, never looked at any of these things very well. Since I figured Pa ran off and left us, I didn't have much interest in what he left behind."

He handed the watch to Deborah. "This is yours now."

"He must have stolen it from Pa—killed him and then took the watch."

Jake shrugged. He looked miserably at Deborah. "I don't know. It's possible, I suppose."

She stared at Jake, realizing that whatever she might think of the father, she had come to care for his son. She wanted desperately to believe that he knew nothing about what happened to Pa.

"We've got to get back to the mine and see if we can find any clues." *Or a body cleverly hidden,* she thought miserably.

Jake nodded. "It would be hard to live with the fact that my pa killed his partner. But if he did, I want to know."

She reached up to kiss him on the cheek and he wrapped his arms around her. "We're in this together, Jake. Whatever we learn about your father won't make me think less of you. If you haven't seen him since you were a boy, then none of this can be your fault."

She handed the watch back to Jake.

"I'd like to keep this here for now. I don't want to lose it in the mine."

Jake put everything back in the package and stowed it in the drawer.

Then they walked together to the mine, each imagining the dark, fearsome fate that might have befallen Ed Palmer up in the ravine.

It took them two more days to shore up the mine and reach the place where the men had stopped tunneling. They studied it carefully, running their hands along the walls, examining mallets and iron chisels that sat at the work site as though the men planned to return.

Jake lifted the lantern and fingered a thin vein of silver. "Why would they stop when they were still working a lode of ore?"

Deborah shook her head. "I don't know."

"Neither do I. My father was a lazy man. I can't believe he murdered a hard-working partner before the vein was exhausted."

Deborah nodded. "It doesn't make sense. But at least we know we can get some silver to offer a reward."

"That's true. But it's too late to start tonight. We'll start tomorrow," Jake said.

As they walked back, Jake kept a possessive arm around her waist until they reached the outskirts of town.

"Have I told you that I would rather work a mine with you than go to a dance with any other gal?" Jake asked.

Deborah laughed. "And I'd rather work a mine with you than take a buggy ride with another man, especially the man I took them with."

Jake squeezed her waist. "It's his loss. He didn't know when he had a good thing."

"It worked out for the best."

She believed that now with all her heart, thanking God each night for preventing her from marrying Timothy. Compared to Jake, he was as exciting as a mud hen.

"Maybe we were meant for each other," Jake suggested.

She smiled up at him. In spite of her fatigue, her heart fluttered with excitement. Could it be that she had found not only a mining partner but a lifelong partner, a husband to love and to cherish?

She smiled up at him. "Time will tell."

"If I can keep Oscar from sweeping you off your feet in the meantime."

She began to giggle. The mental picture of Oscar struggling to lift her was ludicrous. He would stagger and stumble. And drop her. It was more likely she could pick him up.

"What's so funny?"

"Oscar carrying me off. I'm not small, you know."

"Oh, yes?"

"Yes."

A mischievous glimmer filled his eyes.

Before she realized what he was about to do, he bent and in a swift motion scooped her into his arms. She shrieked and threw an arm around his sturdy neck.

He grinned at her. "There. That was hardly any effort at all."

She had to admit that she felt entirely secure, pinned firmly against the hard muscles of his chest. She laughed and struggled playfully.

"Put me down before someone sees."

"Only if you promise to let me be the only one to hold you."

You're the only one who could, she thought. But she answered, "I promise. Now put me down."

He set her gently on her feet.

A man leading his mule team out of town gave them a quick look before moving on.

"We'll be a scandal," she said.

"A town's boring without a little scandal."

"I'm not sure Carrie would agree."

"Then I'll put on my best manners. Let's stop and get that watch. You can take it home with you."

They stopped by the jail and got the watch. Deborah held it clutched tightly in her palm as they walked back to the boardinghouse. They said good night, and Deborah turned to go inside. She was startled when Oscar appeared at her elbow.

"What's that in your hands?"

"My father's watch. It was in the package that Jake got. The one you told me about."

Oscar pulled at his slim mustache. "That sounds like he wanted his son to have the murdered man's possession. Maybe he and Jake were in on it together."

Deborah frowned at the little man. "Then why would Jake show it to me?"

"I don't know. Maybe he forgot it was there."

"I think you're looking for an excuse to blame Jake. He hasn't heard from his father since he disappeared."

"Are you sure?"

"I believe him."

"Then I think you're in for a cruel surprise."

Deborah shot him a withering look before she turned and stalked into the house.

She stumbled to the kitchen the next morning, half awake and aching from helping Jake with the mining. Pete handed her the newspaper. The headline read: SHERIFF CAUGHT WITH MURDERED MAN'S POSSESSION.

Deborah groaned. "When I get my hands on that little weasel, I'll wring his neck."

Carrie raised a brow. "Why did he write such a thing?"

"I made the mistake of telling Oscar that Jake had Pa's watch," Deborah explained.

"Just because it was in the package doesn't make him guilty," Pete said, fuming.

"He's just looking for something to sell papers. But I'm getting tired of what he writes about Jake. It's like he has something personal against him," Carrie said.

Deborah knew the reason. But she kept it to herself. Oscar had staked an early claim on her and resented Jake's success. It angered her to think he would stoop so low, or think it would get him what he wanted.

Pete's expression was grim. "I think it's about time Oscar found himself a new place to room."

"I think you're right," Carrie agreed.

Deborah hated to see them lose the income. Yet, she would not be sorry to see him go. She was tired of feeling to blame for the things he wrote about Jake.

She wondered what Jake was thinking. He'd surely seen the story by now. And she would have to wait all day to see him and wonder if he would be angry with her for leaking the information about the watch. He might not even want to work the mine anymore.

He finally arrived an hour after supper, looking tired.

She hurried out to greet him. "I'm so sorry, Jake. When Oscar saw me looking at the watch I told him it was in your package."

Jake ran a hand through his sandy hair. "It's not your fault. But thanks to Oscar, I spent most of the day meeting with the town leaders, convincing them that I didn't know where the package came from or anything about a murder. I think it's smoothed over now."

"Good. I promise you I won't speak another word to Oscar. And Carrie and Pete are going to ask him to move out."

"They won't have any trouble finding someone to take his place."

Deborah's eyes sparked. "Well, I'll be glad to see him go. He uses his pen to attack anyone who offends him."

"The power of the press." Jake smiled down at her, lightening the mood.

She took his arm and they walked together to the mine.

When they arrived, Jake plunged ahead with the lantern. Deborah followed. She had to force herself every step of the way down the hundred yards to the end of the damp and musty tunnel. Yet once they shone the light on the thin line of silver, she felt her discomfort dissolve.

She stood back as Jake swung a pickax he'd taken from the entrance to the mine. Another ax lay near Deborah's feet. She picked it up, intending to relieve him when he got tired. A thick red liquid was smeared on one side of the ax. It caught her eye and she stared at it. Slowly it dawned on her that it looked like blood.

"Jake. If this is blood, then I've found a clue."

Her hands shook as she handed Jake the ax. She imagined her father, back turned to his partner as Jake had been to her, working away on mining the silver. Had Roy Taylor come from behind and used this ax to murder her father?

Her knees felt too weak to support her. She leaned against the cold earthen wall for support.

Jake examined the ax closely, running his finger along the dried blood. "It's blood, all right. But it's not a clue to our mystery. This blood is barely dry. I'm guessing somebody came in here since we shored up the tunnel. Probably killed a rat while they were inside."

Deborah glanced around. Though she didn't see a rat, she felt a little easier about the blood. Yet why had someone come into *their* mine? "Do you think someone's been watching us work?"

"Probably just a drifter who came in for shelter and out of curiosity wandered to the end of the tunnel. I doubt we'll see any more of him."

Deborah shivered. "I hope not. After all this work, I don't want someone else jumping our claim."

Jake set down the ax and kissed her solidly on the mouth. "We won't let that happen. I promise you."

It was slow going getting ore from the thin vein in the rock. Kathleen took a turn while Jake paused for a drink. "How long do you think it will take us to get enough to offer a reward?" she asked.

"At this rate, about a month."

She felt disappointed. She had imagined they would go in and in a day or two have what they needed. She sighed, wishing there was an easier way to get the money. But her wages from Carrie were small and, out of those, she sent a little home to help Ma. They would just have to keep swinging.

She moved aside as Jake took up the chisel. He swung the mallet, driving the chisel into the rock and sending small bits flying around them. "Too bad this is such a small vein," he said.

"Maybe we'll find more."

"You never know. It could be buried deeper in the rock."

Deborah sincerely hoped so.

They broke off for the day with a small bag of ore.

"We might as well work a few more days before we take this to be crushed. This doesn't contain enough silver to be worth the trouble yet," Jake said.

She followed him from the mine.

He paused and scowled at the ground. "I didn't notice these when we came here, but there are footprints. Someone's been here, all right. And some of the prints lead to the lean-to. You wait here while I check it out."

Deborah felt as though her heart had jumped to her throat as she watched Jake draw his gun. As he crept toward the shelter, she felt the terrible fear of having him gunned down in front of her. She shivered and knew right then that she didn't dare plan a future with him. A sheriff was always in danger. She would never know when he would leave her one day, never to return. Yet, she also knew, from the way her heart beat with fright, that she loved him.

He hesitated beside the door before throwing it open and stepping inside. Deborah edged closer, desperate to see what was happening. Nothing made a sound except for the heavy scrape of his boots on the rocky earth. She took a deep gasp of air and realized she'd been holding her breath.

Jake stepped out of the shack. "Someone recently made coffee. Left some in the pot. Whoever it was must have moved on."

"I'm so glad. I was worried when you went in there alone."

Jake holstered his gun. He put his arm around her shoulders and drew her against him. "I should be glad to have a pretty woman worry over me. Only I don't want you to worry. I want you to be happy and comfortable all the days of your life. And if I can, I'll see to it that you are."

Was he suggesting they spend their lives together? She glanced up quickly, trying to read his face. But he didn't meet her eyes.

She wondered what she'd say if he did propose. She knew that being the wife of a sheriff wasn't a recipe for mental peace. With every fiber in her body she dreaded losing a man early in life, as her mother had done, and raising her children alone. No, it was better they remain as they were.

When they parted at the boardinghouse, Deborah planned to get cleaned up and then go to her room to spend the rest of the evening with her treasured books.

She was pleased to see Oscar piling his things from his room into the upstairs hallway.

"Are you moving out?"

"Yes. If your aunt and uncle think they can censor what I write, they've another thought coming. They're so in love with the sheriff that they can't see his faults. And if I were you, I wouldn't keep company with him. You'll see.

It'll turn out he knows all about the murder. He'd probably murder his partner too. But since nobody wants to listen, I'm taking a room above the newspaper office. It will be quiet, and I'll save myself the rent."

Deborah tried to hide her irritation with his accusations. "I hope you'll be happy there."

"I will."

He took her hands. "This doesn't mean we can't still be friends. I'd like to take you to another concert. Will you come?"

"I don't think so."

She pulled her hands away and drifted down the hall, leaving him to stare after her. She'd been struck by a sudden thought that made her forget all about Oscar. What if Roy had returned to the mine and Jake didn't know it? He might have been holed up in that shack.

She would give a great deal to speak to Roy Taylor. And it made sense that if he'd spent all his money, he'd return here to his mine, hoping to make more.

She sank onto her bed, knowing exactly what she must do. Jake had to stay in town tomorrow to guard the gold shipment. But she could slip out after supper and head to the mine. She would find out for herself whether Roy had come back. The worst that could happen was that she would find it deserted and see that Jake was right about there being a passing drifter. But if Roy were out there, she would find him. And she would make him tell the truth.

The next morning it was a relief not to have Oscar pestering her to keep company with him. He had moved his things out and slept at his nook above his office.

Old Joe still puzzled her, though. For someone who had

been so friendly early in their acquaintance, he hardly said a word to her now. She'd asked Pete to find out if she'd hurt the old man's feelings. Pete reported back that Joe had said his feelings weren't easily hurt. So Deborah had gone on being polite to him, though he ignored her.

Late in the afternoon, just before time to start supper, Nancy dropped by with Kathleen in tow. Carrie took the child and shooed the young women out of the kitchen. "I've got a morsel of gingerbread that Kathleen can chew on while I roll out these biscuits. We'll have ourselves a fine time."

"She makes a fuss over Kathleen every time she sees her. She likes children, doesn't she?" Nancy asked.

Deborah looked thoughtful. "I never thought about it. Carrie and Pete never had children of their own. But I suppose she must like them. She passes out cookies to the boys who play ball in the lot behind us."

They settled into the porch swing, and Nancy looked as though she was about to burst with news. "The most wonderful thing has happened. You'll never guess, so I'll tell you. I've been invited to join the Women's Club. They meet at the Beaumont Hotel. And this Friday, Mrs. Wright is going to treat us to lunch. I've never been inside the hotel dining room, but I hear it has Roman windows and an orchestra gallery in the dining room."

"How wonderful! I bet you'll have the best time of your life."

Deborah already understood Nancy well enough to know that she thrived on social engagements, especially when they included influential citizens. And she loved to admire fine things. No doubt she'd come back with a detailed account of the hotel and everything inside. Just on hearsay, she was doing a pretty good job of it now, and she hadn't even been to the hotel.

Suddenly, Nancy broke off prattling and stared at Deborah.

"You must think it's awfully rude of me to come here and share this when you weren't invited. But that was only because the ladies don't know you. As soon as I'm established there, I'll make every effort to see that you become a member too." She patted Deborah's hand.

"It's all right, Nancy, really. I don't have time to go to meetings. And I'm not sure I'd like to go if I had the time."

"Well, you'll have time one of these days. A girl like you won't stay single long. For a while I thought you and the sheriff might make a pair. But after I saw that terrible story about how he kept your pa's watch, I knew you'd have nothing more to do with him."

"He didn't know it was Pa's watch. Someone sent it to him, along with his pa's things, years ago."

"I wonder about that, don't you? Who would have sent them to Jake?"

"I wish I knew. Maybe they could tell me what happened to my pa."

She was sure Nancy would think it was far-fetched to believe that Roy was still alive. If he were, wouldn't he have kept his things? Yet it niggled in the back of her mind that just maybe he wanted everyone to think he was dead.

It was worth a walk to the mine even on the slightest chance that he had come back.

When Nancy gathered Kathleen and headed home, Deborah joined Carrie in the kitchen to help with supper.

"That Kathleen is a cute one," Carrie said. "I always

wished I'd had me a girl. Maybe you'll marry and settle somewheres around here, and I could have me some babies to play with."

"I hope you're not in too much of a hurry. I haven't had any proposals yet."

"I know of one man who likes you pretty well. And for your part, you couldn't find a finer husband."

Deborah feigned surprise. "I didn't know you were so fond of Oscar."

Carrie swatted at her with her dishcloth. "Poo. You know who I mean."

"If you mean the sheriff, he hasn't proposed either."

"Just give him a little more time. I can tell he's taken with you."

Carrie's words both pleased and worried her. She'd lost one man in her life. She didn't want to chance losing another. She knew she loved Jake. And deep in her heart she trusted him. He was not the kind of man to keep quiet about a murder, even if it involved his own father. At least, she didn't think he would. She wondered what she'd do if it were her own father in question.

After supper cleanup, she grabbed her bonnet and started for the door. Carrie called from the parlor, "Going off somewhere with the sheriff again?"

"No. He has to work tonight. I'm taking me a walk."

She strolled through town, heading toward the mine. Her heart beat swiftly as she left the edge of town and climbed up the ravine. She had a clear view of the lean-to and of the mine that lay a few yards away.

She listened for sounds of human activity. There was no sign that anyone had been back to the mine. A squirrel scuttled to a tree.

Deborah edged closer. It seemed her instincts about Roy had been wrong.

She eased over to the mine and paused to find the lantern. It was just outside the opening. She frowned. She was sure they'd left it inside.

She lit it and forced herself forward. She might as well do some digging while she was here. The sooner they got enough silver, the sooner they could offer a reward.

She hadn't taken three steps when men's voices rose from the lean-to.

"I tell you I saw someone go in," said one.

"Then it must have been ol' Sully's ghost," said the other.

They were coming out and heading for the mine. There was no way to get away without being seen.

"We can't have nobody skulking around," said the first man.

Deborah grabbed the pickax from beside the entrance. Whoever they were, they didn't sound friendly. She raised the ax and pressed herself against the side of the tunnel. Her heart thudded painfully in her chest as she waited to see what would happen next.

Chapter Seven

A squat, beefy man with a dark, unkempt beard stopped short at the entrance to the mine. His green eyes, narrow and cold, widened in surprise when he saw Deborah.

"Seems we have us a little lady, or should I say a big lady? What are you doing out here all alone, darlin'?"

The tall, thin man who was with him leered at her. His grin showed missing teeth.

"I'm not alone. The others are in the mine," Deborah lied, as her heart pounded against her ribs.

The man started forward. "Now you know that's a fib. We only seen you come in here. You put that ax down and come out so we can show you a good time."

Deborah raised the ax over her head and swung at him with all her might. The ax caught the supporting timber above her head; the momentum of her blow jerked it loose, releasing a cascade of rocks in a cloud of dust. Deborah gave a cry as the rocks pelted her back and shoulders, bruising her. She stepped back, but not in time to avoid the blow that struck against her temple, sending her into a black void as she crumpled to the ground, oblivious to the dust and tumble of the falling rocks.

The men shouted at the blocked entrance to the mine and got no answer. The stocky man sighed and said, "Let's get us some supper. If she's dead, then we're saved the trouble of killing her. We'll dig her out later when we get the treasure."

The tall man looked disappointed, but he followed his companion back to the lean-to. Soon a column of smoke drifted from the stovepipe in the roof.

Deborah drifted slowly to consciousness. Her head ached, and her throat felt parched. She opened her eyes to see a small finger of sunlight poking through amid the fallen rock. She tried to remember what had happened, but she had such a bad headache that it was hard to think. She touched her temple, seeking the source of her pain, and frowned as she drew her hand away. It was sticky with blood.

Then she remembered the two menacing men, her attempt to protect herself. How long had she been unconscious?

She had to dig herself out of here. But first she had to be sure the men were not waiting for her.

She inched herself to the pile of rocks. Every ounce of her bruised body protested.

She listened for voices or for the sound of someone digging at the rocks. She heard nothing except the muffled sound of birds singing their evening songs.

She would have to be quick in case the men decided to come back.

She pulled at the rocks, but the weight of the pile held them wedged in place. And her head ached abominably from her effort.

Where was that iron chisel Jake had been using for mining?

She made her way along the walls of the dark tunnel to the back of the mine and felt in the darkness until she found the chisel. It was heavy in her hand as she lugged it back to the rockslide.

She wedged it between the rocks, ready to pry. Then, from the other side, she recognized the voices of the men. They sounded so close that she knew they must be squatting in front of the rocks.

"What do we do with her?"

"If she's dead, we'll bury her up in the rocks with that no-good skunk that tried to cheat us. Imagine him coming here and trying to dig up the gold and run off with it. I made sure he turned round and saw it was me before I shot him. Knocking over that bank in Santa Fe was a piece of cake. But thanks to this clumsy female, we gotta move these rocks before we can get to the back of the tunnel and dig that gold outta the ground."

Deborah saw the pile shift as they pulled at the rocks. Her heart thundered, knowing they would come into the tunnel, determined to do away with her. She tried desperately to think of a way to hide. There was nothing but earthen walls and hard-packed dirt beneath her feet. There was no place to hide from armed robbers. And a pickax would do her little good in defending herself, even though it had bought her a little time.

She shivered in the clammy coldness of the mine and wrapped her arms around her body. She heard the men dragging at the stones, and she saw the pile shift downward. Cracks between the rocks showed her that night had fallen. It was nearly as dark outside as it was inside the mine. A tiny pinprick of light showed from the men's lantern.

Deborah backed farther into the tunnel, hiding herself in the ebony shadows. She cringed as the pile shrunk, and she could now see the night sky above the tops of the rocks. At this rate, it wouldn't take them long to enter the mine.

Someone yelled. The men ceased their steady scraping. Had a comrade come to join them? If so, she would be doomed even sooner.

The newcomer sounded closer as he shouted, "What's going on?"

She recognized Jake's voice and cried out a warning just before a shot rang out. Other shots followed as Deborah scrambled up the rocks, trying to see out. But the men had taken off into the darkness for cover.

On the next shot, someone screamed in pain, and Deborah's heart went to her throat. If Jake died trying to rescue her, she would never forgive herself. Then she reminded herself that if Jake died, these men would kill her too.

An eerie silence followed the blasts of gunfire. Where was Jake? And where were the bandits?

"You got them, Jake. They're both down."

It sounded like Pete.

Deborah shouted, "Be careful. They're robbers. They stole gold from the Santa Fe Bank."

The shouting made her head feel as though it would split. Yet she had been alone in the dark for so long that she was desperate for rescue.

Jake spoke on the other side of the rocks. "Are you hurt, Deborah?"

She was filled with relief that he was all right. "Not badly. Please get me out of here."

"Step back. I'll have you out in no time."

"Let me help," Pete said.

"You're hurt. Better see to that arm."

"It's just a scratch. I'll be all right."

The men worked with more urgency than the robbers. In a short while, she saw their heads appear and then, after a few more minutes, their shoulders. By the time they were waist high behind the rocks, Deborah began to scramble out. Jake reached out to catch her under the arms and pull her over the top of the wall.

She clung to him weakly, feeling as though her legs had turned to rubber. He clasped her to him for a moment, and then held her out, looking for injuries. But it was too dark for a thorough assessment.

"I caught a rock on the head," she said, pointing to her temple. "Are you hurt, Uncle Pete?"

"Just a nick on the arm," Pete said. "It'll heal in no time."

She shivered. She was beginning to feel chilled and sick to her stomach from the headache and excitement. "And those men?"

Jake pointed. "Both dead. Over there, but don't go look."

Deborah made out the faint outline of bodies near the lean-to.

"I'd better get you both back where Carrie can have a look at you," Jake said.

Pete brought the horses, and Jake helped Deborah onto the saddle before swinging up behind her. He wrapped her in his coat, and they started off for town.

As they rode, he asked, "What do you know about those men?"

"I heard them talking after my pickax caused the rock-slide. They robbed a bank in Santa Fe. Apparently there was a third man, who double-crossed them. They killed him and buried his body up in the rocks somewhere. They were going to bury me there too."

She felt Jake's arms tighten around her. "Not while I have breath in my body."

"How did you know where to find me?"

"Carrie got worried when you were gone so long after dark. It's going on midnight, you know. So she sent Pete over to get me. At first I couldn't think where you might be. Then I decided you must have come out here. It occurred to me there might have been an accident. It didn't occur to me you had company."

Deborah shivered. "When I heard you shout to them, I was afraid they'd kill you."

"It's lucky for both of us that Jake is a quick aim. He drew and shot them both before they got off more than one shot apiece," Pete said, riding alongside them.

"I'm glad of that," Deborah said.

She felt her head begin to droop. An overwhelming fatigue was creeping over her. Her eyes fell shut as the steady rhythm of the horse's gait lulled her to sleep.

She didn't awaken until they pulled the horses to a stop at the boardinghouse. Carrie came dashing out. "What's happened? Is she all right?"

"She got a bump on the head. Best get her inside where we can see to it," Pete said.

"Pete got winged. He needs looking to also," Jake added.

Deborah moaned as Jake dismounted. She wished she could have gone on riding with him forever. She had been comfortable there, warm and sleepy. Her head began to ache as he lifted her from the horse. Overtaken by exhaustion, dizzy, and with legs like rubber, she wanted to lie down.

Jake sensed her weakness and swept her into his arms. She snuggled against his warm chest while Carrie went ahead to hold open the door.

While Pete tended the horses, Jake took the stairs to Deborah's room and deposited her gently atop her bed. Carrie turned up the lantern and bent over her. Deborah shut her eyes against the sudden brightness.

"Yes, that's quite a bump. I'll need water and soap to sponge it off."

Jake took off to fetch the supplies, glad to have something to do.

Soon, Pete joined Carrie. He bent over Deborah to get a look at her.

"She's awful pale."

Carrie glanced up at him. "What happened?"

"She was trapped in her pa's old mine by a rockslide. And it was a good thing too, because there were bank robbers on the other side. Jake shot 'em both dead."

Carrie's hand flew to her mouth. "Bank robbers at Ed's mine? What was Deborah doing there?"

"It seems she and Jake have been shoring it up with the thought of bringing out silver. Deborah wanted to offer a reward for information about her pa."

"That's why she's been looking so tired."

Pete sank onto the side of the bed, looking tired himself.

"As for you, Pete Turner, you get that shirt off and let me have a look at your arm."

Jake returned with the water and soap. Carrie found soft cloths and sponged off her patients' wounds. Jake hung around to watch, a worried frown on his brow.

"It really is just a scratch. It should heal all right if we keep it clean," she told Pete as she cleaned his arm. "You get on to bed and get some rest. I'll sit and watch Deborah for a while."

Pete, fatigued by the excitement and the late hour, seemed more than willing to obey his wife. He plodded off to bed, leaving Jake with Carrie.

"Do you think she's all right?" he asked.

"It's a pretty big bump, but I think she'll sleep it off and feel better in the morning. Why don't you get some rest and come by first thing to check on her. I'll pull up a chair and look after her."

Jake nodded. He seemed reluctant. "If there's nothing else I can do . . ."

"Not a thing."

"It all happened so fast. The men started shooting, and I shot back. Then I realized Deborah was trapped in the mine. I didn't know how long she'd been there or what they might have done to her. It was the most awful feeling I've ever had."

"I know, Jake," Carried said softly. "I know you care for her."

Jake heaved a sigh as he turned away and disappeared into the dark shadows of the hall. He doubted he would get much sleep. His mind kept going over what might have happened if he and Pete hadn't come along when they did.

As it was, she'd been badly injured. Part of him longed to stay and watch over her. The other part was furious with her for her stubborn independence that almost got her killed. Why couldn't she have waited until he was free to go with her?

He kicked at a rock and wondered if it was wise to have allowed himself to care for her. The price of love could be very high. Survival was hard for a woman in the West. Life was fragile and easily snuffed out, whether she was a sturdy and strong-willed woman like Deborah or a small and frail woman like Ma. The memory of his mother haunted him. He carried an aching soreness of heart from watching her slow decline. Would losing his heart to Deborah cause him sorrow someday?

Yet what could he do? He thought of her so constantly that it was hard to keep his mind on his work. He could never be happy without her. But could he be happy with her and with the worry she would bring him?

In spite of his restless spirit, he slept soundly until the first light of day. He rose and ate a quick breakfast of corn pone before going out to saddle his horse. He wanted to stop by and check on Deborah before heading to the mine to recover the bodies of the robbers. Then he'd send a telegram to Santa Fe and tell them about the shoot-out.

He let himself in the back door of the boardinghouse and went quietly up the stairs. He rapped softly on Deborah's door before entering.

The room was filled with a pale, early-morning light. Carrie looked to be dozing in her chair. Deborah's eyes flicked open and she smiled as Jake approached. She reached out her hand, and he took it.

"How are you feeling?"

"Better, thanks. I'm sorry I put you and Pete in danger."

"You couldn't have known about the bandits." His sandy brows drew into a frown. "I could lecture you about going out there all alone. *That* was not a smart thing to do. Promise me you won't do that again."

She shook her head and then winced at a stab of pain in her temple. "You don't have to worry about that."

"I'm going out there to get the men's bodies. I'm hoping the bank will know who they are. I wonder how much they got away with."

"They said the gold was buried in the back end of the mine."

Jake brightened. "I'll take a look. It would be nice to recover it."

Deborah frowned. A new worry obscured the pain of her cuts and bruises. "Are you sure you should go alone? How do we know there were only three of them? What if the rest of the gang rides up while you're in the mine?"

He gave her fingers a gentle squeeze. "I'll be extra careful and keep my gun at the ready. I won't let anybody sneak up on me."

She looked unsure. "I know you're good at your job. I could tell that last night. But those men were so cold and ruthless. If they trapped you in there and saw you'd killed their partners . . ." She broke off with a shudder.

"I tell you what. I'll come back in three hours with or without the gold. If I don't, you can send a rescue party."

She smiled up at him. "I'll hold you to it."

He leaned down and kissed her gently on her pale lips. "You get some rest. You're still looking a might peaked. And I've been wanting to invite you on a picnic at Box Springs."

"Really?" Deborah brightened. "When?"

"Soon as Carrie says you're well enough to go."

"I'll be fine by Thursday."

He gave her a big grin as he turned for the door. "If

determination can make you well, I don't doubt you'll be on your feet by then."

He walked away, still wearing a grin.

Carrie continued to pretend to be asleep. She squinted one eye for a look at Deborah. Judging from the smile that lingered on her niece's lips, those two were headed straight to the altar.

Jake rode out, leading a horse to carry the bodies. He wondered if he'd find the stolen gold. The robbers must have come along Thursday after he and Deborah had left. When they didn't find anybody living in the rickety lean-to, they probably thought the mine was deserted or that the owners were away, No doubt they expected to be in and out before anybody got back.

He rolled the dead robbers in blankets. Then he carried his lantern to the back of the mine and looked around for evidence of fresh digging. The area had been carefully packed down, too carefully packed down to match the surrounding ginger-colored ground.

He took up a shovel and with a few vigorous strokes uncovered two bags of gold. He lifted one in each hand and decided they weighed a good fifty pounds apiece. These men could have lived well on their stolen gain. If Deborah hadn't come along, they would have got away with it too.

He carried the gold from the mine and then peered into the bags. What would it be like to have so much money, to be able to buy whatever you wanted?

He sighed. With as little silver as this mine was producing, he wasn't likely to know. Yet since he'd never had much money, he wasn't going to miss it either.

He tied the bags closed and secured them to his saddle. Then he lifted the bodies onto the horse and lashed them securely in place. Before he left, he wandered up into the rocks to see if he could find the spot where they had buried their companion. After a brief and unfruitful search, he gave up the effort. One way or another, justice had been served.

The sun was warm on his shoulders as he led the horse slowly toward town. Overhead, fluffy white clouds chased across a turquoise sky, playing hide-and-seek with the sun.

His mount nickered and sidestepped where the trail narrowed between imposing gray rocks before opening into a meadow of lush grass and colorful wildflowers. In less than a heartbeat, he drew his gun, alert to the possibility of ambush. If there were more robbers, this would be the perfect place for them to lie in wait.

A jackrabbit dashed past, a blur of long ears and gray fur as he disappeared into the meadow grass. Jake was intensely conscious that the rabbit might not be the only creature hiding at the edge of the ravine.

He dismounted and led his horse. He was a big man and a big target. Atop a horse, he would be hard to miss.

He edged forward, keeping a keen watch while riding through a grove of aspen. He was glad when nothing stirred except the gentle breeze that rustled the bell-like leaves as though they were a thousand chimes.

He reached the safety of town and left the gold at the bank for safekeeping while he dumped the two men with the undertaker, a dark little man of few words.

A quick look at his pocket watch told Jake he had time just to compose a quick message and send it by telegraph to Santa Fe before keeping his promise to Deborah.

He hurried through the rest of his business and came to the boardinghouse just before the three hours were up. He found Deborah sitting up in bed, dressed in a royal-blue bed jacket of soft cotton that brought out the rich brown of her eyes. Her hair flowed softly over her shoulders in fluffy chestnut waves. She smiled up at him and set the cup of tea she'd been drinking on the nightstand.

"I'm so glad to see you," she said in a breathless rush. "I worried the whole time you were gone."

He crossed the room in two strides and leaned down to claim her lips in a warm and lingering kiss. He had just broken it off to sit beside her when Carrie poked her head inside the room.

"Don't tell about the gold yet. I want to hear. I'll be right back."

Deborah flushed at what could have been an awkward moment if Carrie had come a few seconds sooner.

"Did you find it?" Deborah asked.

Jake nodded. "Just where you said, in the back of the mine."

"And those men? They're all dead?"

He took her hand and gently rubbed her fingers. "All of them. You don't have anything to worry about."

Carrie hurried back, dust rag in hand, and took the chair beside the bed. "What did you find, Jake? Was there gold?"

He nodded. "Two fifty-pound bags."

Deborah sucked in a sharp breath. "That's a lot of gold. The bank in Santa Fe will be glad to get it back."

"I sent them a telegram just before I came over. I'm sending the gold on the next armed stagecoach. I'm going to try and keep it quiet that it's going out."

"We won't tell anyone," Carrie said.

"I'd appreciate that. A few folks saw me bring it into the bank. The fewer who know, the more likely we are to avoid a robbery attempt."

Carrie chuckled. "I'm afraid the town may already be buzzing about those men you brought in. It's near impossible to keep a secret around here."

Jake shook his head. "I'll do my best to keep off the rumor mill."

"I'm afraid people never tire of gossip. It grows until it's lots more interesting than the truth," Deborah said.

"And more harmful too," Jake said.

Deborah bit her lip. She had been the cause of most of the gossip that had plagued Jake lately. She determined it wouldn't happen again. There would be no more thoughtless words tossed in public from her lips.

Jake turned to Carrie. "How is the patient? Will she be up to a picnic next week?"

Carrie nodded. "If she rests up like I tell her, she'll be fine as a fiddle in a few days."

Jake's eyes sparkled as he looked at Deborah. "That's good news, because I'm not a good enough cook to pack the picnic basket."

Deborah lolled against her pillow. "And you expect an invalid to do it?"

He laughed. "Careful. If you're too convincing, she won't let you out of bed."

Deborah sat upright, squaring her shoulders to military attention. "Is this better?"

Carrie rolled her eyes. She pushed up from her chair and said, "I've got work to do, so I'm leaving you two to work out the picnic."

She swatted Jake's leg with her dust rag and said, "Only

don't you be staying too long and wearing her out. Five more minutes, that's all."

She left them to settle their plans.

"I thought we'd go Thursday, on your afternoon off," Jake said.

"I'd like that. I'll fry us up some chicken and bake some biscuits. If you're really lucky, Carrie will let me bring along a pie."

"You really don't mind making the food?"

"Not at all. It will give me something to look forward to. And planning it will keep my mind busy."

He ran a finger tenderly along her face. "*You* keep my mind busy. I think about you a lot."

Deborah captured his hand and brought his fingers to her lips. "And what do you think?"

"I think you're the most beautiful and exciting woman I've ever met."

She clasped his fingers to her cheek and said, "And you are handsome and brave, just like a knight out of a fairy tale."

"Then let me be your knight. Just don't be watching when I fall off my horse."

Deborah laughed. "You're just the sort of humble knight that I like. I do a lot of falling myself."

Jake leaned over and kissed her on the forehead. "I have my orders to be out of here and let you rest. But I'll be back on Thursday, so you'd better be well."

She grinned. "You can count on it."

She kept smiling after he left, humming a merry tune she'd learned as a girl and planning out the food for their picnic. She looked up, curious, when someone rapped on her door. Her smile faded as Oscar slipped inside, looking guilty for having slipped in behind Carrie's back.

Chapter Eight

I left a few things with Joe. I came by to pick them up," Oscar explained. "He told me you were laid up. And I also heard that the sheriff brought some men to the undertaker. You know what happened?"

Deborah glowered at him, incensed that he had the nerve to sneak into her room.

Instead of being put off, Oscar said, "I heard he shot them in a poker argument."

She leaned forward, her eyes shooting sparks. "You wouldn't print such a lie."

"Some folks say it's the truth."

"Well, it's not true."

A sly grin spread beneath his mustache. He had tricked her into confessing that she knew what had happened. She resented him for his underhanded methods.

He pulled out pen and paper and sat down next to the bed, though he'd not been invited. "Who were those men?"

"If you must know, they were robbers, hiding out after their robbery. I stumbled across them when I was out for a walk. To escape, I ran into an old mine. My reckless haste caused a cave-in, and I got hit on the head. Jake happened along, and they shot at him. He killed them both and rescued me. So, you see, he's actually a hero."

Oscar leaned forward so far that she thought he might fall out of the chair. In fact, she hoped he would. But he maintained his balance and asked, "How many men were there?"

"Two. A third was already dead. They killed him when he double-crossed them."

"Where's the gold?"

She gave him an impatient grimace. "Do you think robbers would walk right up and tell me where they hid their gold?"

He frowned. "I suppose not. Maybe it was in the mine."

"I didn't see it. But it was dark after the cave-in."

"Where is this mine?"

"I'm still new here. I don't know my way around very well."

It was as much truth as he was going to get. She wasn't about to tell him about how she and Jake had been mining their fathers' old claim together.

He sighed. "I would like to have seen that mine." He put away his pen. "Oh well, I have the true story, thanks to you. I knew I could count on you to help me out."

"I only did it to keep you from writing any more lies about Jake. What you did before was wrong."

His shrug conveyed his lack of remorse. "I write what I see. And I see that you've gone soft-headed over the sheriff. Maybe you're the one who doesn't see the truth."

"Jake's a fine man."

"He's overbearing and uncivilized." His voice turned softer as he said, "It's a shame you've never been exposed to the cultured cities of the world, where there's grace and charm. Had you learned to appreciate the polish and beauty of genteel manners, I'm sure you would have favored a gentleman over a rough sheriff."

Deborah nearly laughed aloud, realizing he was speaking of himself. "Have you ever been to Paris, or London, or New York, perhaps?"

His cheeks flushed with color. "No. But I've been to Denver. And it's a great deal more refined than here."

He slid his chair back and stood. He soothed his ruffled feathers by saying, "I have an idea of why those men were here. I'll bet Roy Turner was one of them. I'll bet he turned to a life of robbery when the silver he stole from your father ran out. He led those men back here to a hide-out and got murdered when he tried to double-cross them the way he did your father. The other two men are dead because Jake didn't want them to tell how his father was one of them."

In answer to her horrified expression he said, "Don't you worry. I won't be printing my opinion of this. I'll stick to the story you told. But you can bet that when I can prove it, I'll print the whole ugly truth."

He turned and left, sneaking out the way he'd come in, a slip of a man who would make his living snooping in doorways. She disliked him more than ever now, most of all for shaking her confidence in Jake.

True to his word, Oscar stuck to the truth, though he could not resist a jab at Jake. His article began: *On Friday evening, Sheriff Taylor had the pleasure of killing two bandits who held Miss Palmer captive.*

The article was short and occupied only a corner of the second page of the paper. Deborah was sure he regretted not having evidence to print a more sensational story.

She brooded on his suggestion that the third robber might have once lived in Ouray. He concluded by saying that the sheriff could use help in identifying the men.

Deborah couldn't help wondering if Jake knew them. Though she hated to admit it, Oscar's accusation had wedged in her mind. It made sense that Roy would have led them back to hide out in the mine.

She wished there were some way to get to the truth.

By the time Jake came by for their picnic on Thursday, she admitted to herself the painful truth. She didn't entirely trust him. She would have pleaded a headache and stayed home except that she had insisted she felt fine while she spent the last three days helping Carrie. If she didn't go, Carrie would worry that she'd let her go back to work too soon.

There was no excuse to be found in the weather either. The few puffy clouds that dotted the field of blue looked as though a giant hand had laid them for decoration. Beams of sunlight danced across the weathered birch beams of the porch. The scent of Carrie's climbing rose filled the air.

While Carrie chatted with Jake, Deborah slipped into the kitchen to get the filled picnic basket. She had spent part of the morning frying chicken and baking biscuits. Carrie had been more than happy to give her a jar of berries for the pie and chilled tea in a jar. In exchange, Deborah had baked two extra pies for the boarders.

The comforting scents of the meal still lingered in the room. And Deborah lingered too. She hated her suspicion that Jake knew about Roy, and she dreaded confronting him. And yet, it would also be difficult to hide her mistrust.

Nonetheless, she couldn't stay in here forever. A few minutes more and Carrie would come looking for her. She sighed deeply and picked up the basket. She would have to make the best of the situation.

Jake took the basket as she joined him, his wide, square fingers brushing against her hand. For a moment, she forgot her doubts and enjoyed the warmth of his touch. Then reality set in, and she warned herself not to be taken in. She had waited all her life to find out what had become of her father. She couldn't let a handsome blue-eyed man derail her efforts and steal her chance to learn the truth.

They walked along companionably through the crowded streets, staying on the boardwalks to keep Deborah's shoes out of the mud. A sprinkling of morning rain had dampened the ground, and the grind of wagons and horses' hooves had turned it to muck.

Their conversation was simple and constantly broken by the greetings of people they passed. It seemed as if Jake knew everyone in town. She supposed that was to be expected from a sheriff.

When they reached Box Springs, they climbed up for a look at the magnificent falls. What Deborah saw took her breath away. Just above them, a thunderous waterfall plummeted into a narrow cavern to crash into white foam at the bottom.

"Drops eighty feet." Jake leaned down to speak into her ear.

"I've never seen anything like this. I'm used to lazy streams. I've never seen such power before."

She had to speak up to be heard above the falls. The cool mist rose about them, forming tiny droplets on her cheeks. She was awed by this display of nature. As a child, she had often wandered along their lazy brook or watched her brothers pull a fish from its waters. Yet she had never wondered about the journey of the water. To think that her pokey stream might be the result of a thunderous waterfall intrigued her.

The sun cast a purple tint on the rocks, making the cavern a fairy wonderland. She would have felt completely enchanted when Jake put his arm around her waist if not for the uncomfortable doubts that Oscar had planted.

He pulled her close and murmured, "A beautiful lady in a beautiful place."

Her heart ached with a confusion of emotion. She gazed up and said, "Have you said that to all the women you've brought here?"

Jake's brows drew together in surprise. "No, though I won't deny that I've come here with a lady before. But I've never told anyone else the things I've told you. I've never felt for anyone the way I feel for you."

Deborah felt a rush of chagrin. She believed that he truly loved her. But did he love her enough to grant her the truth, no matter what the cost to himself and his father?

"I'm sorry, Jake. I know you meant it."

She concentrated on the waterfall, trying to shut out all other thoughts from her mind. She wanted to have a wonderful time today, to make wonderful memories for years to come. Instead, she was tortured by worry about Jake's honesty.

"Let's walk down to the bottom of the falls. It's beautiful there too," Jake suggested.

They followed the trail down to the breathtaking view of the full height of the falls. Jake smiled down at her. "How would you like to have our picnic here?"

There was no one else around in the middle of the afternoon. They spread a worn blanket under a towering pine and settled next to each other. Deborah pulled out the picnic fare. Jake exuded praise over each item she unwrapped until Deborah felt as though she had brought cuisine from the finest French restaurant.

She laughed. "You haven't tasted it. I hope you won't be disappointed."

He captured her fingers as she unwrapped the napkin that held the biscuits.

"I've tasted your food. Why do you think I've been going to all the trouble to court you and do all that work in the mine?"

"So it's my cooking, and not me, that you want."

The light banter eased the tension that had plagued Deborah since they'd set out. Perhaps she could get through this outing without blurting out her distrust. If he were guilty of shielding his father, he was not likely to admit it, anyway.

Instead of releasing her hand, he brought her fingers to his lips. "You have fine-looking hands. Long fingers and smooth skin."

Deborah had never considered her hands attractive. Like the rest of her, they had always been large—masculine, she thought. She had grown up hiding them in the folds of her skirts to keep the other girls from commenting on them. Unfortunately, it hadn't always stopped them.

She met Jake's eyes and felt her heart lurch. There was such sweet and honest admiration in them that she wondered how she could be so foolish as to doubt him. He was well thought of by the majority of the townsfolk, including her aunt and uncle. Why couldn't she just push her foolish doubts aside and give him her trust as well as her heart?

"You make me feel dainty and pretty. That's a gift that no other young man has ever given me. I'll treasure it always."

Pushing aside his fears about whether he would always be able to keep her safe and well, he said, "I'd die a happy man if I could keep you content for the rest of your life."

She blinked at him, wondering if he were hinting at a proposal. How would she answer? Her heart was hopelessly lost to him, and yet her mind was uneasy.

He leaned over and kissed her gently. The warmth of his lips sent tingles down her spine. She was amazed that such a strong, muscular man was capable of such tender kisses. He deepened the kiss as he pulled her firmly against his chest. She could feel the solid beating of his heart.

She clung to him, wrapping her arms around the pillar of his neck. He possessed her lips, exploring every curve of her mouth. And she responded, letting her heart rule, enjoying the sheer pleasure of his touch.

For the length of the kiss, she was completely his, lost to all reason, to anything except how right she felt in his arms. She would have traded nearly anything to enjoy these kisses, this man, for the rest of her life. Anything except the truth about her father.

When he drew away, he chuckled and said, "I guess I got carried away."

Deborah set out the rest of the lunch. She was glad his attention was drawn to the food and not the tears that she blinked back as she poured both of them a tall glass of tea.

They leaned against the tree trunk and began to feast. Jake ate with relish. Deborah forced herself to eat and found that, despite her confused heart, she had a healthy appetite.

Jake smiled as he watched her neatly devour a drumstick. Here was a woman who was not afraid to show that she was human. Some girls would pick at their food, pretending that they never ate more than a mouthful, when he knew good and well they went home and had their fill. He liked a woman who was honest about her appetites, all of them. And Deborah was as honest about her stomach as she was about her heart. He didn't believe she would have kissed him back if she didn't feel affection for him. If only he could get over his fear that he would lose her as he had lost Ma, he would ask her to become his wife.

He mulled it over as they lingered after lunch, watching the clouds play chase across the deep blue sky. If he gave into his fears for her and let her get away, wouldn't he always worry what had become of her? If *he* married her, he knew he'd do his best to watch out for her. He'd give his very life to keep her safe. And even if a life together broke his heart someday, he couldn't bear the thought of giving her up.

He glanced at her, debating whether he should share his feelings. Her expression was pensive. She blinked her dark lashes and swallowed hard.

"Is something wrong?"

She started and drew a deep breath. "No. I'm getting a little drowsy. Maybe we should walk."

He thought she looked more sad than drowsy, but he didn't say so. He helped her pick up the remains of their picnic and load it into the basket. Then he took the basket and said, "Why don't we find one of those hot springs? You said you wanted to soak your feet."

She smiled and his heart lifted. "That would be fun."

He led the way to a small pool of water, out of the way

and rarely used by the people from town. It sat in a meadow surrounded by wildflowers and green grass. Deborah remembered the times back in Kansas when she'd slipped away for a dip into the stream to cool off. She reminded herself that this water would not be cool.

They sat on rocks near the pool and peeled off their shoes and socks. Jake rolled up his pants, and Deborah hiked her skirt to her calves. She cringed, knowing just what her mother would think of such behavior.

They waded in, and Deborah breathed a sigh of pure ecstasy. It was warmer than she had imagined. As she walked, the water swirled about, bathing her muscles in a delightful massage. Jake had waded in farther. It was knee-deep in the middle of the pool. In spite of his efforts, his pants were getting wet.

With the modicum of modesty she possessed, Deborah knew she couldn't raise her skirts any higher. So she contented herself with a walk around the rim of the pool. The mud and rocks beneath her feet felt like silt. The rocks were polished smooth, and they were slippery. Deborah took a misstep and slid, flailing her arms for balance.

As she pitched backward, Jake rushed toward her, lost his footing, and fell face forward into the pool. He looked up to see her sitting waist deep in the water, her skirt spreading around her like a mushroom cap. The startled expression on her face was priceless. He knew he would remember it forever.

"Are you hurt?" he asked.

Deborah shook her head. "Only my dignity."

Jake grinned as he rose to walk over and sit beside her. "How about mine? I intended to come to your rescue like a knight in armor, and I fell into the water."

She leaned back on her arms, making no attempt to rise. "It feels really nice. I hadn't intended to have a soak, but since I'm already wet, I might as well."

Jake roared with laughter.

"What's so funny?" She raised her brows, genuinely perplexed.

"You're the most practical woman I've ever met. I love it."

"And you, sir, are just as practical. Notice that you're sitting right beside me."

"Maybe so. As you said, we are already wet."

She glanced around. "I just hope no one comes along. I'd never live it down. *Crazy Deborah,* they'd call me."

"Nobody comes here except the Indians."

"How did you know about it?"

"A Ute friend of mine showed it to me a long time ago. We played here as boys."

"You were lucky to have a friend to share your fun."

Her wistful tone made him wonder if she'd had a lonely childhood.

They soaked until the warmth of the afternoon sun and the heat from the pool flushed their faces a bright red.

"We'd better get out and start to dry. We both look like lobsters," Jake said.

He stood and offered her his hand. She grasped it and allowed him to help her to her feet. She felt bottom heavy from her wet petticoat and skirt.

"You're right. We'll need some time to dry. If we walk back into town both dripping wet, there'll be no end to the speculation."

As they walked across the meadow, Jake carried the picnic basket in one hand and reached for her hand with the other. "I've had a wonderful time being with you today."

She nodded. "The waterfall was wonderful, and I'll never forget our accidental soak in the hot spring."

"Neither will I. Perhaps when we're old and gray and rocking on a porch, we'll talk about them."

Deborah bit her lip. She wanted nothing more than to plan a life with Jake. But for two good reasons, she didn't dare. If she married a sheriff, she would always wonder if he would come home each night. And, more immediately, she wondered if he were hiding recent contact with his father.

He glanced down at her. "You're awfully quiet. Did I say something wrong?"

"No. It's just that . . . well, I don't know if we can be together on that porch."

His sandy brows drew into a frown. "Why?"

She hadn't planned to blurt it, hadn't wanted to do anything to ruin their day, but it came unbidden. "I'm uneasy about what happened at the mine the night I got hurt."

He pulled her to a stop in a grove of aspens. "Uneasy about what?"

"What are the chances that the bandits would have come to our mine? I mean, who would have led them there? But if your father was still alive and had spent all the silver, he might have been one of them, the one they killed."

He stared at her, struggling to make sense of her accusation. "Anybody could have stumbled on the mine. It was just chance."

Deborah looked away. "I wish I could believe that. I wish I could be sure that you didn't know your father would be there. I can't help wondering if that's why you tried to keep us from working last Friday night."

"I had a gold shipment to protect."

"Did you really? Surely you can see how suspicious it

could seem. What if you realized those men killed your father and you shot them to keep them from telling that he was there?"

He put his hands on her shoulders and turned her to face him. She stared up into his blue eyes. They were dark with fury.

"All this time we've worked side by side and you still don't trust me? And I don't see how I can do a blame thing to change it. Not if you're determined to shackle me to the sins of my father. It's like a curse I can't escape."

Deborah blinked back tears. "I don't want to believe it. Really I don't. I don't know what to think."

The hurt of her suspicion pierced as sharply as an arrow through his heart. He couched his pain by withdrawing from her, his face like flint, as hard and cold as a statue. In a frosty tone, he said, "I think you're right. There's no future for us, not when I have to prove my innocence anew every day."

Tears coursed down her cheeks. This was not what she wanted. Answers, yes, but not to lose Jake. Yet, she knew they couldn't build a relationship on anything less than complete honesty. She couldn't pretend to trust him. To do so would lead to disaster. If it didn't come between them now, it would come between them later.

"Come on. I'll walk you back."

Deborah sniffed. Even angry, he was still a gentleman. "I can find my way back."

"I'd feel better seeing you safely home."

Their earlier closeness had evaporated. Deborah plunged ahead, taking no enjoyment in his company. Though he walked only a foot away, they might as well have been miles apart.

They stalked along having no conversation until they reached the boardinghouse. When Jake followed her to the door, she said, "You needn't see me inside."

"I'm not seeing you inside. I'm looking for Pete. He knows what Pa looked like. I figure he can take a look at that body. Then I'll have a witness when your half-baked rumor spreads all over town."

Deborah felt her hackles rise. Was he likening her to Oscar, who enjoyed nothing better than to spread damaging rumors about the sheriff?

"I have no intention of spreading any rumor. It was Oscar who thought of it, so if it spreads, you can thank him, not me."

"So *he* put that idea in your head. I would have thought you knew better than to listen to him."

"Well, I guess I'm not as smart as you thought."

Pete strolled into the hall. He'd just washed up for supper. He caught sight of them and grinned. "Nice afternoon for a picnic."

His grin faded as he noticed the tension on their faces. "Something wrong?"

"Deborah thinks my pa was the third outlaw, the one the others buried. I'd like to have you go out with me after supper and take a look at the man they buried."

Pete frowned, letting his gaze rove from Deborah to Jake. "You think Roy was an outlaw?"

Deborah sighed. "I don't know what to think."

Jake's narrowed gaze chilled Deborah. "After I get proof, it won't matter what you think. We're gonna find us an Indian and uncover that grave."

Chapter Nine

Deborah managed to get herself up to help Carrie finish supper. They laid out the meal for the guests and retreated to the kitchen to their own supper. Carrie and Pete didn't press her for details about what had gone wrong. Still, she noticed that Pete pulled at his whiskers all through the meal while Carrie chewed on her lip and cast Deborah worried looks.

Finally, Carrie exploded. "I wish you'd tell us what went wrong with you and Jake. Pete said he came in here like a thundercloud, talking about digging up a grave."

Deborah sighed. She knew she could hardly keep it a secret. After all, Jake was sure to have told Pete everything she'd said.

"I told Jake that someone had suggested that his father was one of the outlaws. It makes sense that he would bring them to his old mine to hide out. And if Jake knew they'd killed him, he might have killed the other two to make sure they didn't tell."

Carrie's frown grew into a deep crevice. "Who suggested such nonsense? Jake never killed anybody to keep them quiet. He killed those men because he had to. And if he'd known his pa was one of them, he would've owned right up to it."

Deborah felt like sinking into the floor as she heard Carrie's unalterably good opinion of Jake. "Oscar suggested it. It seemed possible at the time."

"Well, it's dumb as an ox. I can't believe you fell for it. I never heard of anything so foolish. And now that poor boy's got to prove he didn't cover for his pa."

"When he does, I suppose I'll owe him an apology."

"You will. For your sake, I hope he can accept it."

Deborah didn't need her aunt to tell her she'd made a mistake. No doubt Jake would find the grave. And if he did, and she was wrong, he'd never forgive her. And she would deserve it for listening to Oscar.

She'd insulted Jake and disappointed her aunt and uncle. She felt as though she hadn't a friend left in the world. And suddenly it was all too much.

Blinking back tears, she said, "I'd like to go upstairs if you don't mind."

Her last glimpse was of Pete, sitting at the table and shaking his head.

Jake met up with Pete at the stable and they rode out of town together. It was a fine evening for a ride. The heat of afternoon had given way to the refreshing coolness of an alpine evening. The sunlight danced playfully across the craggy faces of the mountains, which curved round the valley like a mighty fortress, painting them in hues from rosy pink to soft lavender. On any other day, Jake would have taken pleasure in the view. Now his thoughts were on one thing alone. He was going to prove the third man wasn't his pa.

A small part of his heart beat a little quicker with the worry that Deborah might be right. Could Pa have joined up with the outlaws? While he'd never admired Roy Turner, he'd never believed he could turn bandit. But now he wouldn't rest easy until he knew.

"How you figuring to find the grave?" Pete asked.

"I don't figure I *could* find it. It's up in the rocks somewhere. I have a friend that can track a butterfly through the air. I've asked him to help us."

Pete grinned. "I don't reckon he could track butterflies, but I hope he can find this grave. I won't be much help. I've never been any good at tracking."

"If anybody can find it, Red Deer can. We played together as boys. He built a little cabin for his family in a grove down by the river. He fishes and traps to get by."

Pete frowned. "I haven't seen Indians around these parts in a long time."

"Red Deer keeps to himself. He gets along better that way. Still, he didn't mind doing a favor for an old friend. He's meeting us at the mine."

Red Deer was waiting when they rode up. Pete eyed him a little warily. Red Deer's face showed no expression as he acknowledged them with a nod. Only his eyes, dark and piercing, were alive in his somber face.

Jake swung from the saddle and greeted him. The contrast in the men was striking. They were nearly the same height, yet Jake was stocky while Red Deer was lean. Jake's blond hair glistened in the sun when he swept off his hat to wipe his brow. Red Deer wore a band around his head to hold his long black hair in place.

Yet he and Jake spoke like brothers, and soon Pete felt at ease.

Red Deer pointed up the rocky slope. "I found where they went up. This way."

Jake grabbed a shovel and the blanket he'd brought to wrap the body. Then he followed Red Deer. Pete, pained by the arthritis in his knees, lagged behind. They scrambled up rock and stunted tree growth to a spot that leveled out.

Red Deer ran the toe of his boot across the ground. "Men dug here. Not long ago."

"This has to be it," Jake said.

He shoveled carefully, not wanting to damage the body. It was a shallow grave, carelessly dug. It wasn't long until a pair of worn boots showed beneath the dirt. Jake uncovered the rest of the body, brushing the dirt off with the branch of a stunted pine.

"I can tell well enough to know he weren't your pa," Pete said.

"No, he's not Pa," Jake agreed. "He's much too short. I'm taking him to the undertaker. With your witness and a few more who knew Pa, we can stop the rumor that Pa was in on the robbery."

Pete helped him wrap the body and carry the remains down to the horse.

Jake turned to Red Deer. "Thank you, my friend. I couldn't have found the grave without you."

"And I wouldn't be alive today without you."

Jake nodded without reply.

The men clasped arms in a gesture of farewell.

"Tell Meadow Song and your little ones hello," Jake said.

"It's been a long time since you've come to see us."

"I'll come again soon," Jake promised.

"I'll tell Meadow Song to make her buckwheat bread."

Jake laughed. "She's a mighty fine cook."

They swung onto the horses and when they looked again, Red Deer had disappeared into the trees. As they rode back out of the narrow canyon, Pete asked, "What was that about saving his life?"

"Nothing, really. We were children, young and foolish. We decided to climb a rock face, over there."

He pointed. His eyes scanned the distant cliff, reliving the memory. "I got to the top. Red Deer was nearly up when he lost his footing and grip. He was forty feet above the ground, hanging by one hand. I crawled past the edge of the cliff and hung over as far as I could. I grabbed his hand and pulled him up. It's lucky I've always been heavier than Red Deer. If it had been me hanging there, he'd have gone down with me. I had nightmares for months about losing my grip on his arm."

Pete nodded. "I guess he'll always feel in your debt."

"I wish he wouldn't. He's paid it off in friendship."

"But that's not how he thinks, is it?"

Jake shook his head. "I guess not."

It was growing dusky by the time they reached town. The street's lights winked a welcome as they rode through. The few people who were still out stared curiously at the blanket-draped body.

The blacksmith, who was closing his shop for the night, stopped them to ask, "Who you got there, Sheriff?"

"Last of the three bandits. They'd buried this one after they killed him in a falling-out."

The blacksmith tipped his hat. "You did us proud, catching those men."

"Thank you, Walter. Some of it was pure luck."

"That don't take away the fact that you done it."

As they rode on to the undertaker's, Pete said, "That's the kind of gratitude I like to see."

They left off the body, and Jake headed home. He'd have his witnesses to prove that he didn't cover up the death of Roy Turner. And that was what counted.

Pete felt bone weary as he climbed the stairs. Carrie had already gone to bed, and he couldn't wait to join her. But first he had an errand that demanded his attention.

He rapped softly on Deborah's door. He was prepared to speak with her in the morning if she were already asleep. But he hoped she wasn't.

Bare feet hit the floor and scuttled to the door. She opened it a crack. Her eyes grew wide. Her hair fell loosely on her shoulders. She was clad in a white robe, and Pete thought she looked like a little girl.

"Come in, please," she said.

Pete shook his head. "I just wanted to tell you that we found the body. It wasn't Roy Turner. I can testify to it."

Deborah caught her lip between her teeth. "I wish I'd never listened to Oscar, though I'm the one who let the doubt grow in my mind. I owe Jake an apology."

"I think you do." Pete hesitated a moment. The light from her room showed the tired lines etched in his face. "It hurt him that you thought he would deceive you."

"I know. I'll talk to him first thing in the morning."

Pete padded back downstairs, leaving Deborah alone with her thoughts. She sank onto the bed, wondering how she could have been such a fool. Why had she listened to Oscar when she knew he wanted to discredit Jake? She knew the answer. It was because she had to be absolutely sure that she could trust him. And she hadn't been able to trust a man in a long time.

She woke early, before time for breakfast chores. She slipped out of bed and dressed before descending quietly down the stairs. She picked up her shawl from the coatrack beside the door and eased out into the early-morning chill.

She felt sure she could catch Jake before he left for work. Her instinct told her he wasn't going to come looking for her. So, she figured, she'd have to go to him.

She took long strides, breathing deeply of the primrose-scented air. There were few people about this early. For that, she was grateful.

Deborah remembered the directions to Jake's house. He'd described it in detail during their long hours in the mine. She would be looking for a small Queen Anne–style home with green trim and a white fence around the yard. He had spent the last few years fixing it up and wishing he could have done more to improve it while his mother was alive.

She turned onto Seventh Street and continued until she was sure she'd found it. It was exactly as she'd pictured it in her mind.

She walked up to the charming wooden porch that wrapped around the house. Now that she was here, she felt her nerves give way. What if he didn't want to see her?

She took a deep breath and rang the buzzer. She had brought this upon herself and there was nothing to be done except face him.

After what seemed an eternity, she heard him turn the

knob. The door creaked open and Jake filled the entrance. He was already dressed in tan cotton trousers and a plaid shirt. Yet from the dishevelment of his hair, she decided he hadn't been up for long.

"Good morning, Jake."

"Morning, Deborah. This is a surprise."

"I had to talk to you."

"You said quite a bit already."

She bit her lip, feeling guilty as charged. "I know I did. And I'm here to apologize. I had no reason to question your honesty. I'll understand if you don't want to speak to me. I'd be angry if I were you."

He studied her a moment, then said, "Why don't you come in for some coffee while I decide what to make of you?"

Deborah breathed a grateful sigh that he hadn't turned her away.

He held open the door and she slipped past him into a cozy parlor, homey yet simply furnished. A braided rug warmed the floor. A cloth sofa of dusty rose and two matching overstuffed chairs sat before a low, polished table. A piano that looked old and well used sat against the far wall.

"This way's the kitchen."

She followed Jake to the back room. She was surprised by the neatness of the shelves that were arranged with cooking utensils, all within handy reach. A pan of mush simmered atop the polished stove.

He poured her a mug of coffee and set it on the little pine table that was set for breakfast for one. She clasped her fingers around the mug and warmed her hands as she sat with Jake at the table.

He leaned back in his chair, his long legs stretching out into the kitchen. "The mush is almost done if you'd like to stay," he invited.

She shook her head. "I have to get back to help Carrie with breakfast in a little while. I just came to tell you I felt bad about what I'd said."

"Pete told you, didn't he?"

She nodded. "It was silly of me to suspect you of covering up for your pa."

"And what about the next time you get fed an idea about me? Will I be suspect again?"

Tears filled her eyes as she met his offended gaze. "I won't listen to Oscar again. You have my word."

"But do you trust me, Deborah? Do you really trust me? I can't go on with these continuing suspicions that you hold against me."

"I'm sorry. I know I haven't been a very good friend. But if you'll forgive me, I won't do it again. I hope we can go back to working the mine and forget this ever happened."

"So that's it, is it? You don't care about how your doubts made me feel. You just want a strong body to help you work the mine. It's good to finally see that I've placed my affections in a one-sided relationship."

It was all Deborah could take after swallowing her pride to come and offer her apology. Her temper sparked and she rose hastily to her feet. "If I didn't care that I'd hurt you, I wouldn't have come here. I've apologized the best I know how. And if it's not enough, then I'll work the mine by myself. And I don't care if you ever come to help."

She whirled and started for the door.

Before she took three steps, she felt Jake grasp her shoulders and whirl her to face him. "You'll mine by yourself, will you? And keep the profit if I'm not there?"

Her mouth fell open in shock. It took a moment for her to absorb the enormity of his insult. Her eyes blazed as she tried to jerk away. "How dare you accuse me of being a thief!"

He held her tightly, ignoring her efforts. When she'd worn herself out, he said, "I don't believe you're a thief. I just wanted you to know how I feel when you doubt me. I guess we're even now."

Deborah sagged, feeling exhausted. Tears coursed down her cheeks.

He reached out and wiped them gently away.

"I trust you. I just want you to trust me."

She allowed him to pull her into his arms.

He whispered into her ear, "Do you think we could start over?"

She nodded, and a small sob escaped.

Jake felt pierced by remorse. "You've been through a lot. I shouldn't have upset you. It was selfish."

Deborah shook her head. "I'm glad we got it all out in the open. I couldn't stand knowing that you must have hated me for what I said."

"I didn't hate you. Haven't I told you that I love you? I think I've loved you from the first time I rescued you from that weasel of a reporter."

"And I loved you too, even when I was mad."

He pulled her close, and she snuggled against his chest.

"Hold me like this forever," she said, "and let's never be mad."

Jake chuckled. She loved the way it rumbled from the depths of his chest.

"I don't think either of us could promise that," he said.

"Maybe not. But I love being comfortable with each other again."

"If we fight, we can look forward to making up."

He tilted her chin and stared tenderly into her eyes before claiming her lips. He kissed her firmly and thoroughly, leaving her in no doubt that his forgiveness was complete.

When they at last pulled apart, Deborah sniffed the air. "Do I smell something burning?"

"Only my breakfast." Jake lifted the pot off the stove. "Sure you don't want some?"

Deborah wrinkled her nose. "Very sure. I have to get back and help Carrie."

He walked her to the door. "Partners again?"

"You bet. I'm not about to do all the work."

He pulled her to him for a last quick kiss.

"Are you up to a little digging tonight?"

"I'm ready. Is seven o'clock all right?"

He nodded. "I'll come by, and we'll walk together."

He grinned as he watched her head down his front walkway and down to the street. Her skirts swished vigorously around her long legs. Here was a strong woman, a woman who could keep up with him. He pushed away the nagging reminder that bad things could happen to even the most vigorous of women.

He shut the door and concentrated on salvaging his breakfast.

As he spooned out the top layer of mush, he had an idea for a surprise for Deborah, a surprise for that very evening. And with a little help from Carrie, he would manage to pull it off.

Deborah was just sitting for supper that evening when Carrie said, "After you eat, I want you to change into something nice. We have company coming over."

Puzzled, Deborah set down her fork. "Company? But I have plans with Jake tonight."

"It won't take long. You can still see Jake."

"Who is it?"

Carrie glanced at Pete to share a sly smile. "You'll find out soon enough."

Deborah glanced from one to the other. She tried to imagine all the possibilities, yet none came to mind. "Please won't you tell me? I don't like secrets."

Carrie grinned at Deborah. "Sorry. I'm sworn to secrecy. But don't look so worried. I promise it'll be a nice surprise."

Deborah felt like balking. She wanted to insist on being let in on what was going on. Yet hearing Carrie's firm tone and seeing the determined look on her face convinced her it would do no good.

She wasn't allowed to help with dishes but was shooed right upstairs after supper. "Wash up and put on that pretty yeller dress with the daisies and white lace," Carrie said.

"I would really feel a lot better if you'd tell me what's going on," she said, trying again.

Carrie shook her head. "Nope. Then it wouldn't be a surprise."

Deborah went through the motions of washing and getting dressed, all the while wondering if someone from back home had come to town. But why wouldn't Carrie have told her if it were Ma or any of the family?

She frilled her bangs and pulled up her hair, leaving two ringlets to cascade from her temples. She pinched her cheeks to add color to a complexion grown pale while she was recovering and slipped into her good shoes, shoes that were scuffed in spite of her attempts to save them from wear.

She arrived downstairs just before the stroke of seven. Carrie met her at the bottom of the stairs. "I was just coming up to get you."

Deborah glanced around. Her stomach felt uneasy. "I'm ready. Where is the mysterious company?"

"You come sit down. You'll find out soon."

Deborah joined Pete and Joe in the parlor. They were seated in the corner, engrossed in a game of checkers. She sat on the edge of the horsehair chair and waited.

A few moments later, Jake stepped into the house. She opened her mouth to apologize for not being ready to go to the mine. Then she noticed that he was dressed in his Sunday best and wearing a brand-new felt hat. He carried a bouquet of wild daisies tied in pink ribbon that were as bright and sunny as her dress.

She stood up as it dawned on her that her mysterious caller had just arrived. She looked from Jake to Carrie. "Would someone tell me what's going on?"

Jake handed her the flowers. "The mine will still be there tomorrow. There's an orchestra and a dance at the opera house tonight. I hope you'll agree to be my partner."

The fluttering in her stomach became a swarm of bees. "I'm afraid you'll be disappointed. I dance very poorly."

"So do I. With me bumbling into the other dancers, no one will notice you."

Deborah smiled. They hadn't been out in public together since he'd asked her out to get ice cream. She hoped it would go better than that disaster.

"I'd be happy to go with you, Sheriff."

"Then grab your shawl, and we'll be off."

Carrie took the bouquet. She was beaming and looking almost as pleased with the surprise as Jake. "I'll put these in water for you."

Deborah pulled her white shawl off the coatrack. She looked back to see Old Joe watching them, a pensive look on his wrinkled face. She smiled at him before she turned away to precede Jake out the door. He took her arm and she felt her heart lift with happiness as they walked into town. A few weeks ago, she was the jilted fiancée of a farmer, ashamed to hold her head up at church. Now, she was headed to a dance on the arm of a man twice as handsome as the one she'd lost. And better yet, he made her feel attractive too.

They arrived at the opera house to find a throng of people filing up the stairs to the second floor where the orchestra was tuning its strings. She ignored the press of the crowd as she clung to Jake's arm.

Her last trip here had been with Oscar in an unsuccessful attempt to find out information about her father. Tonight was pure pleasure, and she intended to enjoy every moment in Jake's arms.

He pointed to the front facade of the building. "This place has a Mesker Brothers cast-iron facade. Fancy, huh?"

"It's beautiful. I love the arches and the scrollwork."

"Ol' Edward made his money at the Wheel of Fortune Mine, the lucky dog. Building the opera house was his wife's idea, to improve our culture."

Deborah nodded appreciatively at the building. "You have a lot more culture here than I had back home. The best we could hope for was a barn dance every now and then."

"You like it here, don't you, Deborah? I mean, you don't want to move back to Kansas someday?"

She shook her head. "I like it here."

His face relaxed in obvious relief.

They reached the stairs, and she said, "I'd be happy to settle here and maybe open a little bakery. I could do all right with breads and cakes."

"If you were busy with a family of your own, you might not need to open a bakery."

Deborah caught her lip. How could she tell him that she couldn't trust a man for support? Look at Ma struggling all these years on the farm. A man could leave you stranded, penniless and with a family. No, a business of her own was a good idea.

"I'd like to have my own shop. The money I could make would help me feel secure," she explained.

Jake pondered what she'd said as they reached the second floor. Somehow he'd make her reconsider. A wife of his would never have to slave all day like his mother, getting worn out and old before her time.

But he wouldn't argue tonight. For now, it was enough that she was agreeable to settling here.

Tonight was for fun. As the music began he took her in his arms, and they started to waltz.

Deborah scanned the crowd as they swirled along and saw Oscar scowling at her from a corner of the room.

Chapter Ten

After three dances in the warm room, Jake suggested Deborah take a seat along the perimeter while he fetched punch. She found Nancy, looking flushed and happy, and sat down beside her. Nancy clasped Deborah's hand. "I'm so glad you're here. I've been wanting to see you again. Tom and I hardly ever get out, but our neighbor offered to watch Kathleen, so here we are. Are you here with Jake?"

"Yes. And I'm having a wonderful time."

"I'm so glad to see you up and around again. I heard about how you were trapped by the cave-in and how it saved you from those awful men. And then Jake came along just like a knight in armor. It sounds romantic."

Deborah didn't remember it being very romantic. It was painful and scary, and she was glad it was over. "It was frightening. Tonight is romantic."

Another tune started, and she watched the women twirling around the room in the arms of their men like bright flowers in a summer garden. The air was scented with perfume and the citrus aroma of the punch. She took it all in, wanting to remember everything about this evening, from the light melody of the orchestra to the excitement of dancing in Jake's arms.

She glanced up to see if Jake and Tom were headed back with the punch. Oscar stepped out of the crowd and blocked her view.

"I was wondering if I might have this dance."

She stared up at him. She could think of few things she would like less than to dance with Oscar. She had an urge to give him a tongue-lashing for the ideas he'd put in her head about Jake's father. But seeing as this wasn't the time or place, she said, "I'm sorry, Oscar. I'm waiting for Jake to come back with our punch."

He fidgeted and glanced over his shoulder. "But I've got to talk to you."

His tone was urgent. His lips twitched nervously beneath his mustache.

"You've already told me quite enough. And none of it was true."

"You don't understand."

"I don't want to understand," she hissed.

"My information was a little faulty, but I'm sure I'm on to something now."

She spotted Jake's blond head above the crowd. "Would you like to tell the sheriff what you're on to?"

"No. But since you can't spare me a dance, I'll call on you tomorrow."

He disappeared into the crowd before she could object.

Jake and Tom returned in jovial humor and presented the ladies with their refreshment. Deborah promptly put Oscar out of her mind as she and Nancy joined in light banter with the men.

After a dozen more dances, the footsore crowd broke up, crowding down the stairs and spilling into the street to make their way home. Deborah and Jake walked for a ways with Tom and Nancy.

"It was fun to get out again, wasn't it?" Nancy asked Tom.

"If you didn't mind my stepping on your feet."

She grinned up at him. "It was worth it."

Tom nodded at Jake. "He looked pretty good out there on the floor. It must have been due to Deborah."

"Yep." Jake draped his arm around Deborah's shoulder.

The warmth from his body sent tingles down her spine. He was strong, yet wonderfully tender. That he returned her feelings was more than she could ever have hoped for. If forced to, she could live on that comforting fact for the rest of her life. It meant more to her than a lifetime commitment from a dozen men like Timothy.

Deborah smiled up at him. "Jake deserves the credit. He held his own out there just fine."

"I think we all did well. If little Kathleen behaved herself, maybe our neighbor will watch her again and we can all go out again," Nancy said.

"We'll find out soon enough," Tom said.

They reached the street where Nancy and Tom turned to go home. They said their good-byes, and Jake and Deborah continued alone. She snuggled against him, feeling chilled in the night air, even with her shawl.

"So you really had a good time?" he asked.

"I had a wonderful time."

"I figured we deserved to have a little fun together. The mine will still be there tomorrow."

"Do you think our work will pay off? I'm beginning

to wonder if we'll collect enough silver to offer a decent reward."

"Don't give up. Tom said what we've found is a decent grade. I don't think we'll strike it rich, but if we keep working, you'll have enough for that reward."

"I intend for us to split whatever we make," she assured him.

They strolled up to the boardinghouse, and he took her hands. "I don't want the silver. I'm hoping for more, much more. I'd give you all the silver in Red Mountain if it would buy a lifetime with you."

Under the glow of the streetlight, she could see his face. Sincerity shone from the depths of his blue eyes. Had she at last found a man she could trust, a man who would not leave her or let her down?

"That would cost you, but not in silver," she said softly. "I could spend a lifetime with you. But I couldn't be happy with only a year or two . . . before a bullet cut you down. I don't want to worry every day that you'll still be alive at the end of the day."

He ran a finger gently along her cheek. "You don't have to worry about me. I intend to live to be an old man, to dangle grandchildren on my knee."

He put his hands on her shoulders as he turned her to face him. "But speaking of worry, I didn't tell you this earlier because I didn't want to dampen the evening. And it's probably not something to worry about, but I got a telegram from Santa Fe today. It seems there were four men who robbed that bank, not three. That means there's still one on the loose."

In spite of his reassurance, she felt her knees grow weak. "You don't think he'd come here, do you?"

"Probably not. Not if he knows the gold's gone. But just to be safe, promise me you won't go to the mine alone."

She gave a weak laugh. "You don't have to worry about that. The last time I went alone turned out badly."

He pulled her to him. "Oh, Deborah, I want to keep you safe always. Safe from bad people, safe from poverty or sickness. If only I had that power."

She nestled against his shoulder. "I think I fear loneliness more than any of those things."

"I can promise you, you won't be lonely. You'll always have me."

"If only you could keep that promise," she whispered, too softly for him to hear.

He walked her up to the porch. Light spilled from the windows. She thought of what it would be like to have her own home. All of the decisions would be her own: what to buy, to cook, and to sew. She would work for herself instead of under the critical eye of Ma or the watchful eye of Carrie.

It was a tempting proposition. Yet, she mustn't let it make her lose sight of her goal. She'd determined to find out what happened to Pa. She wondered if they were to marry, if Jake would still help her in this quest.

He kissed the top of her head and then her temple where her tendril began. He trailed his kiss along her cheek until he reached her lips. His breath was warm and soft. He found her mouth and kissed her with the longing of a man who did not want to leave her and go home alone.

When the kiss ended, he sighed and said, "I'd best get back and let us both get some rest. I hope tonight didn't tire you out."

She shook her head. "Not at all. I feel wonderful."

"Then we'll meet tomorrow and work the mine?"

"I'd like that."

"You're the boss." He grinned and with a parting wave, he turned and walked away.

She stared a moment, savoring the memory of his kiss, feeling torn between desire and the insecurity of life with a sheriff. Could she live with it? She honestly wasn't sure.

Shivering now, she opened the door and stepped into the happy oasis of the patchwork family of a boarding-house.

Oscar popped in the next morning on his way to work. They were just finishing the breakfast dishes and getting ready to sweep the carpets when he walked in with an air of assurance, took Deborah's elbow, and insisted she talk with him in private on the porch.

Carrie scowled. "You don't go with him if you don't want to."

Oscar scowled back. "She'll wish she had, if she doesn't."

Deborah set down her broom. "It's all right, Carrie. I'm sure Oscar will be quick."

She pulled her arm from his grasp and led the way to the porch. "Now what do you have to tell me that is so important?"

He studied her a moment. "Do you know your hair shimmers like polished bronze in the sunlight?"

She rolled her eyes. "Oscar, I didn't come out here for you to talk about my hair. If you don't have anything else . . ." She edged toward the door.

"No, wait. That's not what I came to say. I came to tell you that I was wrong about it being Jake's pa that was killed by that gang."

She sighed in exasperation. "I know that."

"But I'm not wrong about this. Did you know they had four members?"

She nodded. "Jake told me last night."

"That means the last one is still alive. Of course Jake wouldn't kill his own pa. He let him get away."

"Do you never get tired of these ridiculous accusations?" she said, storming at him. "Pete would have known Roy. And he didn't see him there."

"It was getting dark. And Pete's eyes aren't as young as they used to be. I tell you, Roy Turner was the fourth member of that gang."

He drew a breath and continued, ignoring the flash of warning from Deborah's eyes. "I bet that gold never got to Santa Fe. I bet he knew which coach it was on and went and robbed it."

Deborah shook her finger in his face. "You pompous, vindictive little man. Get off this porch and never come back. I don't believe you, and I don't want to hear any more of your wild ideas."

She stomped into the house without a backward glance as the color rose from Oscar's neck to his cheeks. If that was the way she wanted it, that was the way she could have it. He wouldn't try to warn her of the dangers of falling in with Taylor men. She could find out for herself that bad blood ran in that family. He turned away, feeling wounded yet not discouraged. She'd come over to him when she saw he was right. And this time, he felt sure he was.

Deborah and Jake worked the mine the next two days, following the trickle of silver ore. Deborah didn't say a word about Oscar's visit. She put it out of her mind, determined not to believe a word he'd said.

When they finished up on the second night, Jake scraped together their diggings and said, "I'll take these to Tom on Monday and see what he thinks of them. We might have enough now to offer that reward."

Deborah nodded. "I guess then we'll stop mining? It's been a lot of work for what little silver we've taken out."

Jake grinned at her as he funneled the ore into a bag. "I don't know. It's in my blood, you know. Now that you've got me started, I don't know if I can stop. There's always a chance that a rich vein runs just out of sight, maybe down a chimney."

Deborah dusted her skirts as they stepped out into the sunlight. "I could get it out of my blood fast enough. I feel like a mole every time I step into that musty tunnel."

He raised his brows in mock surprise. "I was thinking of taking residence in Pa's old shack. I thought I'd give up being a sheriff and we'd get hitched and work this mine for the rest of our days."

Deborah groaned. "Starve to death, you mean."

"You wouldn't starve to death married to a *sheriff*."

"I might if he were killed."

Jake reached to pull her to him. How could he erase the stubborn set of her jaw? All he could think of was a kiss, a kiss that would unite them, body and soul, and convince her of his love. A kiss that would make them both forget about danger, and hardship, and everything except their desire to be together.

He ran his hand down the back of her dark, tangled curls and tilted her head up to meet his waiting lips. Her lips were warm and pink and soft as the petals of a rose.

He savored the sweetness of her response and the soft feminine feel of her in his arms.

At last, he stepped back and smiled down at her. "Come with me on a walk tomorrow after church. We can pick some of the first wild strawberries."

"I'd love to. If we get enough, I'll make you shortcake."

"Then you can be sure we'll get enough."

They strolled companionably back toward town.

After a while, Jake said, "The undertaker told me he had a stranger come in this morning. He was asking questions about how the outlaws got killed. Said he'd heard about it and was curious. Gus answered a few questions and then told him he'd better go see me if he had more."

"Did he come to see you?"

"No."

Deborah shivered. "You think he was the last member of the gang?"

"I don't know. If so, I don't like the idea of him hanging around town."

"Neither do I."

"Don't worry." He wrapped his arm around her. "I'm sure he'll leave when he learns the gold is gone. And if I find him first, I'll arrest him as a robbery suspect."

She rested her head against his shoulder. "You're right. There's nothing to worry about."

They reached the boardinghouse. Jake kissed Deborah good night. Then, feeling satisfied with their day, he walked back through the cool of the summer evening. He watched the first stars appear and twinkle brightly in the sky. Their sparkle seemed a promise of a bright future. He breathed deeply of the pine-scented air and made a decision. He would give up his fears and doubts and ask Deborah to be his wife.

Never before had he felt a yearning for a lifelong companion. In fact, he had decided it would be prudent to remain unattached with none of the emotional complications of marriage. But that was before he met Deborah.

When she'd been injured in the mine, he'd known the agony of caring for a woman he might lose. He weighed the price of caring about someone so intently that he could barely eat and sleep for worrying about them. Yet he knew that, whatever the price, it could never be as high as watching Deborah wed another man someday. He loved her far too deeply to ever give her up. To give her up would surely be as painful as anything the future might bring.

On Sunday afternoon, Jake brought two berry buckets. He also brought his mother's wedding band in a small velvet-lined box in his pocket. It had been in his family for more than fifty years, belonging first to his grandmother before it belonged to Ma. Now he hoped to give it in pledge to Deborah to hold until they were wed.

He set the baskets on the porch and opened the door. Deborah was waiting in the parlor, looking fresh and pretty in a dress with puffed sleeves and bright blue flowers. She clutched a worn straw hat with a faded blue ribbon. Jake vowed that one day she'd have a passel of new hats to keep the afternoon sun off her face.

As they set off, Deborah chatted about the strawberry jam she'd made each year for the town fair in Kansas. When he failed to reply, she glanced up at him and said, "I'm boring you. I'm sorry. I should know that a man isn't interested in recipes."

Absorbed by thoughts of how he could propose, he

flushed so brightly that it could have been mistaken for sunburn. "It's not that. I like hearing about your cooking. I just wasn't listening as well as I should have been."

She smiled so charmingly that he felt his pulse leap. She was as unspoiled and fresh as snowfall on a virgin slope, and unaware of her beauty and its effect upon him. Her dark eyes sparkled as he leaned and bestowed a kiss on her pert little nose, upturned just enough to be enchanting.

"I promise to be better company. And I can't wait to try your prize-winning jam," he said.

"We grew strawberries at home in the garden. I wonder if the wild ones will have a different taste. I might need to adapt the recipe." She grinned and added, "No matter. It will be fun to experiment."

"And you can call on me anytime to give you my opinion."

They reached the edge of the meadow where the wild berries grew along the creek.

Deborah knelt to examine them. "They're small. Our berries on the farm were the size of apricots. These are little, like peas."

Jake popped one into his mouth. "They're sweet, though. Go ahead. Taste one."

He held out a tiny red berry and placed it in her mouth. Her lips, soft as rose petals, touched his fingers, and he felt a possessive warmth overtake him, a longing for her to become his very own wife to love and to cherish. He studied her lips, her chin, and the curve of her silky cheek. He wanted to memorize every detail of her face.

She glanced up to say, "It is sweet. Small, but just as good as the ones . . ."

She broke off, distracted by his serious expression. A frown creased her brow. "What is it?"

His heart pounded until he was sure she must hear it. He debated pulling out the ring and asking her this very moment. Yet his mouth felt dry as cotton. His thoughts were in a jumble. This wasn't the way he'd planned it. He'd planned to wait until they'd picked the berries and were ready to go home. Since that still seemed a better plan, he smiled and his heart returned to normal as he said, "I like looking at you. You remind me of a picture of the Greek goddess Athena that I saw in a book one time."

"And you remind me of a Viking warrior hero, come to fight off dragons for me."

He glanced up, scanning the sky with exaggerated concern. "That might put me out of a job. I haven't seen a dragon in years."

She laughed and plopped a handful of berries into the bucket. "Then you can be a berry-picking sort of warrior and help me fill these pails."

Jake worked methodically while Deborah flitted eagerly from one plant to the next. She paused every little while to wipe the perspiration from her face. The sun was a scorching bright ball overhead. It shimmered on the mountains, stealing their color and turning them a ghostly gray.

A mosquito buzzed near her nose, and she swatted it away. An itchy spot on her arm told her another had managed a bite. Other insects flitted about. Bees buzzed in and out of the flowers, and tiny flies swarmed near her face. A dragonfly hovered near a patch of wild daisies. She watched him a moment, admiring his tactics as he hunted for a choice meal. The insect world, just like the rest of the animal kingdom, was full of predators and prey.

And so was the human world, she thought with a shiver. The robbers had been predators, preying on the hardworking people who had put money in the Santa Fe bank. For animals and insects, it was the only way to survive. The robbers had no such excuse.

Jake caught her frowning and said, "Are you tired? I know it's awful hot out here."

She shook away her angry thoughts and said, "No. I'm not tired. I've spent lots of afternoons weeding gardens under the Kansas sun. I'm used to the heat."

She was used to the heat, but her hands were not used to the tiny thorns that had pricked her. She was going to have to borrow some of Carrie's special cream to heal them before washday. They chapped easily in this dry climate, and the hot water and soap chapped them even worse.

Little by little they filled the pails with ripe red berries. Deborah looked over the rim and grinned. "I hope nobody else wants to pick berries for jam. We're cleaning off all the berries."

"There's a lot more down the creek. Other places too. I don't think anybody will be in want."

When the last berries threatened to tumble over the top, Deborah stood up and shook off her skirt. Her hair tumbled freely from beneath her bonnet, and her face was flushed a becoming pink.

Jake set the buckets under a tree and took her hand. "Let's walk along the creek a bit and cool off."

Deborah shot a worried glance at their bounty. "What if a bear comes along? I'd hate to lose all those berries."

"We won't go far. I think they'll be safe."

His heart thudded in a quick staccato inside his chest. He wanted to ask her to be his wife. Yet now that the moment was truly upon them, he felt his courage slipping. He shook his head, unable to believe that a man who could face armed gunmen would be anxious about proposing to his girl. Yet no amount of reasoning would calm his racing heart.

He pulled her under an aspen tree. Its leaves tinkled like a thousand bells in the gentle afternoon breeze. His palms were moist as he took her long slim fingers in his own sturdy hands.

"Something's been on my mind, and I won't have any peace until I come right out with it."

Deborah raised a puzzled brow. Her dark eyes grew serious with concern. "I thought you seemed preoccupied today. Tell me what's wrong and maybe I can help."

Jake chuckled. "Oh, you could help."

He took a deep breath and said, "You know I love you. And I believe you love me too. If that's true, then we belong together. Not just for now, but for the rest of our lives. I don't want to ever lose you. It would kill me to see you marry another man."

Deborah's silken brows drew into a frown. "I do love you, Jake. And I don't want to marry another man."

"Then marry me."

He drew the velvet box from his pocket and said, "I'd be good to you always."

Deborah gasped. She expected the day might come when he would ask her to marry him. She just hadn't expected it to be today. She stared at the box as he held it out to her.

"This was my mother's ring and my grandmother's before her. I hope you'll take it as a troth of our engagement."

He drew a silver chain from his pocket. "You could wear it around your neck on this chain."

Her fingers shook as she took the box and slowly opened the lid. A silver band lay lovingly encased. She removed it carefully and held it in her hand. It was dotted with tiny diamonds that sparkled like a dozen glittering suns.

Deborah felt as though she could barely breathe. "It's beautiful."

"Do you really like it?"

She caught her lip between her teeth. "I really do. But, Jake, we should have talked about this. I do love you, but I'm so confused. You know how I feel about marrying a sheriff. I couldn't stand it if you were to die."

He looked into her eyes that were filling with tears. "We'll be dead to each other if you force us to grow old apart. Is that what you want?"

She shook her head and a tear slipped down her cheek.

He took her chin gently in his hand. "This life holds no guarantees. I want us to be together for as long as God lets us, no matter what might happen."

"I want that too. Only . . ."

"You're worried that you'll be left alone like your ma, and my ma too. Well, you won't. Their lives aren't our lives, and we can't let what happened to them make our decisions for us."

She smiled tentatively and fingered the ring. Even as her mind screamed for her to reconsider, her heart made the decision for her. "You're right. I don't want us to be apart. I'll marry you, and I'll try not to worry. But you'd better promise to stay safe and well."

She gave him a shaky grin, and he wiped away the tear that had rolled down her cheek.

"You have my promise. Shall we put the ring on the chain?"

She handed it to Jake, and he threaded it on. She shivered at the touch of his warm fingers on the nape of her neck as he clasped the chain.

He stood back to smile at her as she fingered the ring. A look of contentment had replaced her uncertainty. Perhaps, like him, she felt better now that they had a solid commitment. Every time she felt the ring or glanced down at it she would think of him and the promise they had made.

He kissed her gently and then turned to lead her back to the buckets. "You've made me a very happy man."

"I'm happy too. I never thought it could feel like this."

She thought of her last proposal. It had brought none of these feelings of excitement or happiness.

Suddenly, Jake stopped dead in his tracks and stared into a patch of trees to their right. Deborah stared too. She couldn't make out what worried him.

"Bear?" she croaked.

He edged in front of her, and she felt her breath catch in her throat.

He didn't answer. He didn't have to. She knew they were in danger when his hand closed on the butt of his pistol.

Chapter Eleven

She peered from behind Jake and saw someone moving behind the trees. Could it be the fourth bank robber? Maybe he'd been hiding out in the woods and had seen them. And now he planned to rob and kill them.

He wove between the cover of the trees, edging steadily closer. Jake raised his pistol and stood ready to call a warning. Then before he could speak, a whistle, clear and shrill, the perfect imitation of a birdsong, filled the air.

Jake lowered his weapon and grinned before calling out, "Did you want to see how close you could get without getting shot?"

Red Deer gave up his game of camouflage and emerged from the grove of aspen. "You wouldn't have noticed me if I hadn't spooked that rabbit." He swung the burlap bag he carried. "I guess he didn't want to be my supper. I got a parcel of them in here."

He nodded at Jake and then told Deborah, "He's loud and clumsy as an ox. A while back, I jumped him from behind and he never heard me coming."

She was still feeling a bit shaken from the flight of her imagination. "Isn't that a dangerous game?"

Red Deer shook his head. "That's the reason for the bird call. We each have one."

"Is that so? I've never heard Jake's."

Jake's eyes gleamed as he said, "I do it better than Red Deer."

He proceeded to copy the lilting song of a meadowlark.

Deborah felt her nerves relax as she witnessed their friendly contest. "You could both have fooled me into thinking you were birds. When did you come up with this way of identifying each other?"

"We were just kids, ten or eleven, maybe," Jake answered.

Red Deer's black eyes glinted with mischief. "It made a great warning when we were young. I remember the time we decided to go hunting all night. I had you keep watch while I stole into my father's tent to get a bow. You nearly got me caught when you saw my uncle walking past the tent. You whistled so hard you nearly woke my father and got me in trouble."

"Your uncle did catch us."

"What happened?" Deborah asked.

Red Deer grinned. "He was my father's younger brother. We were always friends. He let us go without saying a word."

"What happened when you came back with the game?"

Jake's smile was abashed. "That wasn't a problem. We didn't get anything."

Deborah tried to imagine the sturdy, tow-headed boy from town and the black-haired, black-eyed Indian youth, as close as brothers, hunting and fishing together. She found she could imagine it quite well.

"Come home with me and have supper. Morning Star will want to meet Deborah. And she's always complaining that you don't come to see us anymore," Red Deer invited.

Jake turned to Deborah. "What do you think? Would you like to see Red Deer's home?"

"I'd love to, but what about Carrie? She'll wonder what happened to me."

"She'll think we ran late picking berries. We won't stay late enough to worry her."

Deborah glanced behind them. "What about the berries? Will they be safe while we're gone?"

"We'll take them with us. Maybe we can share a few with Morning Star in exchange for supper."

Red Deer led the way along the creek. Pine needles cushioned their steps and scented the air with their spicy scent. Sunlight broke through the tree cover, making the ground a patchwork pattern of light and dark. Jake and Red Deer walked in a companionable silence, leaving the rush of the creek to fill the void.

Deborah estimated they'd gone a mile when she spotted a split log cabin nearly camouflaged among the trees. Smoke rose in a wispy plume from the chimney, reminding her of a fairy-tale cottage from childhood stories.

Her palms grew clammy now that they had reached the house. She wondered what Morning Star would think of having a stranger invited to supper. Red Deer and Jake had grown up together, but Deborah was an outsider. Would she be welcome?

Red Deer pushed open the rough-hewn door and announced, "I've brought guests."

A raven-haired Indian woman looked up from stirring a pot. She smiled shyly when Red Deer introduced Deborah.

Deborah smiled back. Morning Star was a beautiful woman. She wore her ebony hair parted in the middle and braided on each side. She was tall and slender, with a smooth olive complexion that made Deborah feel pale. Her high cheekbones and dark, almond-shaped eyes lent her an exotic appearance that Deborah envied.

A round-faced toddler clung to her skirt, hiding his face when Deborah smiled at him. Jake reached down and swung the child into his arms. "You sit with Uncle Jake while your ma finishes supper."

Deborah expected the boy to burst into tears. Instead he gave Jake a wide grin and reached for his shirt pocket. Jake shook his head. "I didn't know I was coming, Little Bear. I'll bring you a treat next time."

He sat down on one of the skins that lay in a circle on the middle of the floor and made faces at Little Bear to make him giggle. Red Deer handed the sack of rabbits to Morning Star and joined Jake on the skins.

Deborah stood uncertainly, feeling awkward around Morning Star and more awkward about joining the men. She decided to offer her help with supper.

"Is there anything I can do?" she asked, hoping Morning Star spoke English.

Morning Star smiled. "You can fill bowls with stew and set them in front of the skins."

Morning Star took a flat bread from the oven and left Deborah to ladle out the stew.

"This smells wonderful."

"It's rabbit stew with some vegetables from my garden," Morning Star answered, looking pleased at the compliment.

"I haven't had rabbit stew since I came here. But we used to eat it in Kansas."

She placed bowls in front of the men, then three more—for herself, Morning Star, and Little Bear. They sat together in a circle, dipping bread in their stew and listening to Red Deer and Jake talk about the best fishing spots along the creek.

Deborah shivered when Red Deer mentioned that he'd seen the tracks of a mountain lion. She was glad she'd not come across one when she'd walked to the mine alone.

After supper, Deborah helped Morning Star clean the dishes while Jake and Red Deer cleaned the rabbits. When they'd put the last bowl away, Morning Star asked, "Would you like to see my garden?"

Deborah nodded. "I had a garden back home in Kansas. I used to work in it every day from spring to fall."

She followed Morning Star to the neat plot that was fenced with wire to keep out the rabbits. Deborah recognized the feathery tops of carrots poking above the ground. She spotted turnips and beans, corn and squash.

"You have the start of a good crop."

Morning Star smiled her pleasure. "It's nice being close to the creek. I've been able to make a little channel to water the garden."

Deborah took a deep breath of the fresh air. "You must like it here."

A frown creased Morning Star's smooth brow. "We do. But there are those who don't think we have a right to be here. When our tribe agreed to move off the land, some believe we should have moved too."

"I hope no one makes trouble for you."

"So do I. Red Deer tells me not to worry. But I do." Her smile held chagrin.

"Maybe you could buy this land," Deborah said.

Morning Star shrugged. "We have no money. Maybe if Red Deer sells enough skins, we might someday."

"Then I'll hope that he does."

A baby began to whimper.

"That would be my little one, White Cloud."

The women went back to the house. Deborah watched with fascination as Morning Star lifted a tiny infant from a blanket in the corner of the room. He had a thick shock of black hair and a round face that was wrinkled and red from crying.

Jake and Red Deer finished with the rabbits.

"It's time we were going," Jake said. He turned to Red Deer. "You have a fine home here and two fine sons." He nodded toward the infant. "That one has a good set of lungs."

"Come back soon. And bring Deborah," Morning Star invited. "It's nice to talk to another woman."

They said their good-byes, and Red Deer walked them out while Morning Star settled herself to feed the baby. Jake dumped half of one of the berry buckets into an empty water bucket beside the door.

"Tell Morning Star to dry these. We'll sample some the next time we come."

"Come again soon. And come fishing when you can."

After they promised to visit again, Jake picked up the buckets and they headed toward town. The sun was a bright ball low on the horizon when they turned away from the creek to enter the valley.

"What did you think of Morning Star?" Jake asked.

"I like her. A lot."

Jake nodded. "She's a fine woman."

"She told me some people don't think they belong along the creek."

Jake frowned. "Some don't. Some of the men who fish down there want them moved off."

"Morning Star was worried there might be trouble."

"Not if I can help it. But I have to say, it worries me too."

Deborah bit her lip, hoping Morning Star and her family would be safe. "It's pure greed, you known. That's why some folks can't leave others alone," she said.

Jake smiled down at her. "You're a wise woman, Deborah, and a compassionate one as well."

She blushed from the compliment. "And you'll be turning my head with your sweet words, if I don't watch out."

He laughed a hearty laugh that warmed her heart. "I'm not worried about turning your head, only about capturing your heart."

"Then you don't need to worry," she answered softly, fighting back the fear that things were too good to last. It was silly superstition, and she would pay it no heed.

She smiled into his periwinkle eyes and felt reassured. Jake was right. They were meant to be together, and nothing from her past was going to scare her away from claiming the happiness that was rightfully theirs.

Carrie was sitting in the parlor when Deborah came in with Jake. Pete and Joe were engaged in one of their frequent games of checkers. Jake greeted everyone and then headed to the kitchen to deposit the berries. Deborah smiled at Carrie and said, "Sorry I'm late. After we picked berries we had supper with Jake's friend."

"I didn't worry, knowing you were with Jake. I figured you got supper in town."

"Actually, we had supper with Red Deer and his family."

Carrie frowned. She glanced toward the kitchen and said in a low voice, "They should have moved on with the rest of their tribe. It was agreed, you know, that they would move out and give us this land."

Deborah was surprised by Carrie's attitude. "I hardly think they could be hurting anything, living by themselves down by the creek."

Carrie shook her head. "I just don't know why they'd want to. It'd be best all around if they just moved on."

Jake returned and the conversation ended.

Deborah knew that Carrie's opinion would not keep her from a friendship with Morning Star. And yet, since she was staying with her aunt, perhaps it would be best if she didn't mention any further visits there.

When Jake left, she lingered in the parlor, helping Carrie with a basket of mending. Suddenly Carrie gasped. "Deborah Palmer, what are you wearing around your neck?"

Deborah grinned at her. "I wondered when you'd notice."

Carrie leaned forward to study the ring. Her dark eyes were wide with excitement. "Is that what I think it is? Are you engaged to Jake?"

"This was his mother's ring. He gave it to me as a pledge of our engagement."

Carrie let out a whoop that got the attention of both Pete and Old Joe.

"Deborah's engaged to Jake. This calls for a celebration. I wish Jake were still here." She turned to Joe. "Do we still have that bottle of wine down in the basement?"

Pete grinned. "I think so. I guess you want me to go fetch it so we can celebrate."

Carrie jumped to her feet. "This seems as good a time as any. I'll get the glasses."

Deborah was left alone in the parlor with Joe. He didn't seem to be aware of her. His eyes were glued to the checkerboard. With his red-checked shirt, he seemed to blend in with the game.

"What do you think, Joe? Should I marry Jake?" She asked it softly, not expecting an answer.

To her surprise, Joe looked up at her. His faded blue eyes were focused and sharp. "He's a better man than his father. I never knew your father, never knew he had a family."

His voice grew raspy. "If I'd known about you, I might have . . ." He trailed off and looked away.

"You might have done what?" she urged.

Joe pressed his thin lips together as though they were the last line of defense against an explanation he didn't want to give. He shook his head. "It don't matter now."

Carrie and Pete returned with the wine, and Deborah put the strange conversation with Joe out of her mind.

They spent a festive half hour sharing wine and slices of cake that Carrie brought in to celebrate the occasion. Several of the other boarders joined them, having heard the festivity. Before long, it resembled a party.

"Will you make your dress?" asked the widow who had taken Oscar's old room down the hall.

"I'm going to try," Deborah said.

"I'd love to help you. I used to be a dressmaker," the little woman offered timidly.

"I would appreciate that. I'm not much of a seamstress. I feel more comfortable in the kitchen baking a pie."

The women congregated to share ideas about the where and how of the wedding. Deborah listened amiably. She had her own ideas, but the wine had relaxed her, leaving her tolerant of the opinions that were pressed upon her.

At last, when the tenants grew tired, they began to drift to their rooms. Deborah was left alone with Pete and Carrie. Carrie gave her a hug and said, "I'm so happy for you. Will you want to be married here or back in Kansas?"

"Here at St. John's. I'm hoping to save enough for Ma and Mary Lynn to come. I don't know that the boys will care."

"Well, you know that Pete and I will help you in any way we can."

Pete nodded as Carrie wiped at the tears that filled her eyes. "You've been like a daughter to us. And I always wanted a daughter. I envied your Ma her girls."

Deborah smiled in return. "You and Pete have been awfully good to me. I'd love any help you want to give with the wedding. But I don't want to put you out."

Carrie clucked. "Put me out? I'm as excited as a peahen that laid a golden egg."

Deborah laughed. "Then I can't think of anyone I'd rather have help me plan and bake and arrange my flowers."

"When's the big day?" Pete asked.

Deborah laughed. "I don't know. We haven't set one yet, but I'm thinking sometime in mid-August."

Carrie rubbed her hands together. "Good, we'll have plenty of time to plan."

"But not tonight." Pete stifled a yawn as he put his arm around Carrie's waist. "Tomorrow's a working day and we have to be up early."

He began to steer her toward their room. "Deborah needs her sleep too."

"I'll be giving it all some thought," Carrie promised as Pete led her away.

Deborah climbed the stairs to her room, suddenly weary from all the excitement.

As she undressed and lay in bed, she tried to imagine life with Jake in his little house. She could see herself in his kitchen, cooking their morning meal, and at dinner, seated snugly beside him at the table. She smiled at the thought of having his boots and clothes beside the bed. Then she sobered at the thought of the one thing she couldn't give up. That was her determination to have some degree of independence.

She'd sell her baking and, little by little, set up a bake shop of her own. Then if the unthinkable happened and Jake were killed, she would not be left destitute.

She shuddered and pulled the cover up around her chin. He wouldn't be killed. They would live long and happy lives. She summoned her determination to put worry out of her mind, closed her eyes, and went to sleep.

They walked hand in hand to work the mine the next evening. She couldn't remember when she'd been so happy. The evening was scented with an earthy smell from the afternoon rain. The wildflowers, drunk with moisture, stood tall and bright, a kaleidoscope of color that covered the landscape. She could be happy coming out here for the rest of their lives if it meant spending time together.

He smiled down at her as she told all about the impromptu party and the many and varied suggestions for their wedding. He chuckled and said, "At least you know you'll have plenty of help."

"That's true. And I'll take them up on it. I'd like to have Ma and Mary Lynn come in time to help plan the wedding. But I don't think Ma will do it. She's tied to that farm."

Jake frowned. "Too bad. It would be a chance for her to spend a happy time with you."

"It's been a long time since any of us spent a happy time with Ma." Deborah bit her lip. She hadn't wanted to dampen their evening with regrets over things she couldn't change.

She smiled. "I won't want for enthusiasm with Carrie around. You should have seen her."

"She loves you, you know."

"I know. She's been great to me. So has Pete."

They'd nearly reached the mine when she said a bit shyly, "We never set a date, you know."

Jake shook his head. A silly grin covered his face. "I was so happy you agreed that I forgot all about a date. What do you think? Would two weeks give you enough time?"

Deborah laughed. "I was thinking of mid-August. There are a lot of things to do, one of which is to sew a wedding dress."

Jake sighed. "That seems like a long time."

"It's only a couple of months away."

"I suppose a few more days won't be too long to wait for a lifetime together."

He drew her to him and gave her a kiss. She felt the warm and steady beat of his heart, so solid and loving. She was tempted to tell him she'd changed her mind and would marry him next week. Yet she knew that would put a strain on everyone who wanted to help, and she could never get Ma and Mary Lynn here in so short a time.

So she returned his kiss with a full heart and looked forward to the day they would walk down the aisle as man and wife. In the meantime, she'd concentrate her efforts on helping come up with enough silver to offer that reward. She wouldn't have much time to work in a mine once she started planning for the wedding.

They carried the lantern to the far end of the mine where they'd found traces of silver. She pried with her chisel while Jake used the pickax to dig into the wall.

"In a day or two we should have enough for a modest reward," Jake said, when he paused to take a break.

"Good, because I don't want to be walking down the aisle with dirt under my nails and bruises from run-ins with rocks."

Jake set back to work with a determination to make this the last two days Deborah would work in this mine. After this, they could forget about mining and get on with their lives.

He chipped hard and straight into the rock, trying to follow the dwindling vein of silver. Suddenly he stopped, wiped the sweat from his eyes, and held the lantern close. This couldn't possibly be what he thought. He fought down a rising excitement.

He swung away, drawing fresh energy in the hope that he'd found a chimney. He remembered what that had meant on Red Mountain. Still, he'd have to be sure before he raised Deborah's hopes. After all, he was no expert on precious elements.

He was so intent on his find that he didn't hear the intruder's footsteps. It wasn't until Deborah gasped and grabbed his arm that he turned to see a man holding a pistol leveled at his chest.

The stranger was short and stocky, with eyes that were hard and cold as cat-eye marbles. A scar ran down his right cheek above the stubble on his chin. He wore his hat pushed back from his forehead in a casual air that was at odds with his expression.

"So, I caught me a couple of rabbits in a hole." His voice was as cold as his eyes.

"What do you want?" Jake demanded.

"I want what you took from me and my men. But I understand that, thanks to you and your pretty friend here, it's gone."

His eyes narrowed, and Deborah shivered.

"You robbed the bank in Santa Fe." Her voice was barely a whisper.

"That's right. And I left my men here to watch over the gold while I went to find us a better hideout till things cooled down. When I got back, I found out my men were dead and the gold gone. I heard all about how the sheriff here was a hero and gunned them down. So I've been watching you two and waiting for my chance to pay you back."

Jake stepped in front of Deborah. "Let her go. It's me you want. I'm the one who shot your men."

"Oh, I'll let her go, all right, all in good time," he said and sneered. "After I take care of you. Before you came along, I was set for life with that gold."

He aimed squarely at Jake's chest. As his finger twitched on the trigger, Jake pulled Deborah onto the ground, shielding her as he reached for his pistol. He was a fast shot but at a dire disadvantage.

The shot exploded as Jake's gun cleared his holster. The impact of the bullet slammed his body backward against the tunnel wall. His gun clattered to the ground. Deborah grabbed for it. Clenching it tightly in her hand, she fired off a shot before the outlaw could re-aim.

Her bullet caught him by surprise. He staggered backward, staring in surprise at the blood that seeped from the wound in his chest. He dropped to his knees and clattered facedown onto the ground.

Deborah dropped the gun from her shaking hand and turned to Jake. A pool of blood stained the ground beneath him from the bullet that had caught him in his side.

"Jake, can you hear me?"

His eyelids fluttered.

She balled his shirt and pushed it against the wound. It was soaked so quickly that she knew she must hurry and get help.

In a daze, she dashed from the tunnel. She looked around. Her deep need made her half expect to find someone waiting to help. The birds flitted among the pines. A magpie paused to scold her. But, except for her animal companions, she was all alone under the orange glow of the setting sun.

A horse nickered. Deborah followed the sound to find the outlaw's bay tied to a tree beside the far side of the shanty. She spoke to him calmly as she whispered a prayer of thanksgiving and untied him. It would take over a half hour to get help if she ran to town. But if she could get Jake on a horse, they could get back more quickly.

She led the horse to the tunnel and tied the reins to a rock.

The outlaw clutched at her skirt as she hurried past. She

tore her hem away and knelt beside Jake. She leaned over him and said, "Please, Jake, we have to get you help. Can you open your eyes?"

He grimaced, yet managed to focus on her. "Are you all right?"

"I'm fine. But we have to get you out of here. Can you stand if you lean on me?"

"I can try."

Jake kept one hand pressed firmly to his side as he clutched her shoulder with the other. Deborah panted with the effort of helping him to his feet. He leaned heavily against her. They took a few halting steps, walking carefully around the outlaw.

"What happened?" Jake said in a gasp.

"I shot him."

He wanted to tell her he was proud and that it sounded like something she would do. But he was beginning to feel lightheaded. He concentrated all of his efforts upon staying upright.

Deborah led him slowly along the tunnel. It took all of her energy to support him. How would she ever get him onto the horse?

Chapter Twelve

Deborah's fingers were numb from clutching Jake. He leaned ever more heavily against her as they struggled along the tunnel. She was bent nearly double by the time they staggered past the opening.

The first thing she saw was a pair of sturdy brown boots attached to the legs of a man. Her breath caught in her throat as she prayed there were not five outlaws instead of four. Neither she nor Jake was in any condition to fight anyone off.

She raised her eyes and nearly collapsed with relief to see Red Deer frowning with concern. "What's happened?"

"The last outlaw cornered us in the mine. He shot Jake before I got the gun and shot him."

They sat Jake on a flattened boulder while Red Deer quickly examined the wound. "It's mostly through the flesh, but he's losing blood. We need to get him back to town fast."

"You take him," Deborah panted. "You're strong enough to hold him on the horse. I'm afraid I couldn't hold him."

Red Deer nodded. They got Jake to his feet. He swayed, barely conscious, as his friend helped put his foot in the stirrup. It took all of Red Deer's strength to heave Jake onto the horse. He climbed on behind and held tightly around Jake as he spurred the horse toward town.

Deborah sank against the boulder, feeling weak as she saw where Jake's blood had stained the rock. She rested her head in her hands for a moment until the lightheadedness that gripped her passed.

She thought of the man left in the mine and shivered. She supposed she had killed him. Forcing herself not to think of it, she got to her feet. Her concern was for Jake, and he was headed for town.

She pushed off from the rock and set off at a brisk walk, drawing strength as her long legs ate up the ground. She ran the last half mile, arriving in town flushed and breathless.

She passed the blacksmith, who was standing outside his barn. "Did you see where Red Deer took the sheriff?" she asked.

"The Injun took him home while somebody ran for the doc."

Without pausing, she dashed across the street, not stopping until she arrived at Jake's door. She flung it open and hurried inside. Red Deer stood at the door to Jake's bedroom. "The doctor is with him," he said.

Deborah peeked into the bedroom and wrung her hands. "Is there anything we can do?"

"Get me more clean towels," the doctor ordered.

Deborah scurried to comply. After she had collected two thick towels, she brought them to the doctor.

Jake lay on his right side. The doc had peeled away his shirt, exposing his broad shoulders and the blood that streaked across his lower back. He took the towels and wet them in a bowl of water, cleaning the wound, then pressing to stop the bleeding.

"Will he be all right?" Deborah asked.

"The bullet entered at an angle. He's lucky it traveled all the way through and missed his left lung. He's lost a lot of blood. Still, if we can keep infection out, he has a good chance of recovery."

Deborah nodded, blinking back tears. The news was good, yet she realized he was a long way from being out of danger.

She watched awhile and then said, "I'll take care of him if you'll tell me what to do."

"Just stay with him and change the bandage twice a day. I've closed the wound, so the bleeding should begin to stop. I'll show you how to keep it clean."

Deborah nodded, paying close attention to the doctor's instruction.

At last he closed his bag and said, "We'll know in a couple of days if he gets an infection. I'm going to leave this medicine. Mix two drops with water for the next few days to help him sleep. He won't notice the pain so much."

Deborah wiped at a tear that threatened to roll down her cheek. "Could you get word to my aunt that I'll be here taking care of Jake tonight?"

"I'll stop by and tell her." He patted Deborah on the shoulder. "He's strong and healthy. Try not to worry."

After he left, Red Deer slipped into the room. "I'll bring you an herb that will help him heal. My people have used it for years."

Deborah faced the tall, solemn-faced man. "Thank you. I don't know what I would have done without you."

Red Deer studied her. "You're his best medicine. Let him know you're here."

Then he turned and left as quietly as he'd come.

She pulled a chair beside the bed and drew comfort from Red Deer's assurance. She brushed back a strand of hair from Jake's forehead and studied his face. He was so very pale.

He stirred under her touch. The doctor had said to insist that he take a drink of water as soon as he could. She watched to see if his eyes opened, but he slipped back into a deep sleep instead.

She sat back in the chair to wait and worry, because that was all she could do.

Red Deer came that evening and brought the herb. He made a poultice, and Deborah helped him apply it to the wound. Jake roused and muttered, "Go away. Leave me alone."

Deborah cringed at the pain on his face as she redressed the wound.

"I'm sorry, Jake, but you've been hurt. We have to help you."

"Feels like my side's on fire."

"You were shot. Do you remember?"

He mumbled something that she couldn't understand.

"He needs a drink," she told Red Deer.

Together, they managed to get a half cup of water mixed with medicine down Jake's throat before he slipped back to sleep.

Red Deer left, and Deborah settled in for the night.

She dozed fitfully in the chair, waking often to check on Jake.

Early in the morning, Carrie arrived, bearing muffins for breakfast. "I bet you haven't had a thing to eat."

Deborah knew it would do no good to protest that she wasn't hungry. She chewed a muffin and realized she was hungrier than she'd thought. While she ate, she told Carrie what had happened.

Carrie shook her head. "Wouldn't you know it? The deputy brought the outlaw back, and Doc says he's going to live to face hanging for robbery and attempted murder."

"Then I didn't kill him?"

Carrie snorted. "I'm sorry to say you didn't."

As much as she despised the man, a part of her was relieved to know that she hadn't killed him.

Carrie stayed to keep her company until it was time to prepare lunch at the boardinghouse. She promised to send Pete over with a meal for Deborah and broth for Jake.

Jake slept the morning away, and when Pete came, he lingered to help her rouse Jake and feed him some broth. When he'd swallowed all he would take, Pete went away after securing a promise from Deborah that she would eat her lunch.

She had little to do after that except sponge Jake's forehead and watch him sleep. That gave her a lot of time to think. Her spirits sank as she faced the hard questions. Could she really marry Jake, never knowing when another outlaw would seek revenge? Could she wonder every morning if it would be their last together?

She cried at the unfairness of having fallen in love with a man who would break her heart, no matter what she did.

At last, feeling worn and spent, she wiped away her tears as she held the ring he'd given her in pledge between her fingers. She knew now what she had to do. Better for them to suffer the anguish of parting now rather than build a life together and have it torn from their grasp.

When Carrie arrived to sit night watch, Deborah had come to a numb resolve. As soon as Jake was well enough, she would tell him. She wasn't foolish enough to believe they could remain friends, because he wasn't likely to ever forgive her. But she had promised herself she wouldn't end up struggling and alone like Ma. And now that she was faced with the choice, she knew even her love for Jake couldn't persuade her to tempt fate.

She slept soundly, worn out from exhaustion.

In the morning, she got up in time to serve breakfast for the boarders and then made up a plate to carry over for Jake. She arrived to find him awake.

"Doc came by a little while ago," Carrie said. "He said there's no sign of infection. Jake ought to be back on his feet in a couple of weeks."

Deborah smiled. Her heart soared with gratitude. She believed much of the credit went to Red Deer for the poultice, but she kept that thought to herself.

Carrie stretched her stiff limbs. "I'll be off now." She patted Jake's shoulder. "You'll be in good hands with Deborah."

Deborah hugged Carrie. "Thanks. You must be exhausted, and you have all your work still to do with no help from me."

"Nonsense. I'm tough. I got along before you were here." She gave Deborah a little shove. "You go take care of that man."

Deborah sat on the chair beside Jake. He smiled weakly at her. "Some sheriff, huh? You had to save us both."

"It wasn't your fault. We were taken by surprise."

He grimaced as he tried to shift around to see her better. "I should have been more watchful."

She smoothed her hand gently along his cheek, feeling the rough stubble of his beard. "It's over now. No need to worry about what we should have done. I just want you to get well."

He reached toward her and touched her face. "How could I help it with such a kind and pretty nurse?"

Deborah's heart ached at the thought of the pain she would cause him. He wouldn't think her at all kind then. She pushed the thought away. She needn't think of it now. She wouldn't have to tell him until he was much better. For now, she would simply make the most of the time they had together.

She spooned scrambled eggs, grits, and sausage into his mouth, pleased to see that he'd regained a healthy appetite. When she finished, they talked a while before his pinched face told her he needed medicine to relieve the pain and help him sleep.

They kept the same schedule for the next few days, with Deborah spending the days with Jake and Carrie coming at night. When Deborah protested that she could sleep beside the bed and let Carrie stay home, her aunt would have no part of it. Carrie insisted that, injured though he was, it would stir up gossip if Deborah stayed the night.

By the end of the week, Jake was sitting up in bed. He grinned when he saw Deborah and blurted his news. "Doc says I can get on my feet."

He was so excited he began to edge off the bed, causing both Deborah and Carrie to scurry to his side.

"Easy," said Carrie. "You haven't been out of bed for nearly two weeks. Take it slow."

They eased him up and he winced as he stood upright. After fending off a spell of dizziness, he walked slowly to the end of the room and back.

By then a cold sweat and exhaustion forced him back to bed. Even so, he assured them he'd be up again before lunch.

He walked so much the first day that he fell into an exhausted sleep early in the evening. Deborah watched him, overjoyed that he was healing so rapidly, yet knowing the time was coming to break the news.

She heard Carrie come in the front door. Before tiptoeing to the parlor, she pulled off the chain and ring and slipped them inside Jake's bureau drawer.

She walked home in tears, feeling bereft without the precious weight of the ring resting against her chest as she strode along. It had cost her part of her heart to make the decision to marry Jake. Now it had cost her the rest to break it off.

The next day dawned so bright that Deborah sat up in bed and blinked into the sunlight. A mountain jay shrieked outside her window, and an answering cry sounded from a nearby tree.

The scent of lilac drifted in from the bushes below and a quiet breeze stirred her curtains. She longed to lie abed all day and avoid facing Jake. Now that he was getting up and about, he wouldn't need her anymore. So like it or not, today was the day.

She dressed with grim determination and headed downstairs.

Carrie had left Jake on his own the last few nights and was in the kitchen fixing breakfast. She gave Deborah a keen look and said, "You feeling all right? You look pale."

Deborah nodded. "Just a headache. It'll go away."

"Maybe I should take Jake's breakfast."

"No. You have work to do. I'm fine, really."

Carrie felt Deborah's forehead. She looked uncertain. "You're not warm, so I guess you're not sick."

"I'm not sick."

To prove it, Deborah grabbed up a platter of bacon and helped serve the boarders. She even managed to choke down a bit of breakfast herself to convince Carrie of her health. Then she fixed Jake a plate and set off for his house. Each step took her closer to her deepest dread.

By the time she got there, she had a headache *and* a wrenched knot in the pit of her stomach.

Jake grinned at her from the kitchen doorway. "I made us some coffee."

She managed a tight smile. "Now that you're up and around, you won't need me to bring you food anymore."

"No. But I sure enjoyed it. It gave me an excuse to wake up and see you each morning. I can't wait until we're married and you're the first thing I see when I open my eyes."

Deborah swallowed hard as she followed him into the kitchen and set his food on the table. He poured them each a mug of coffee. The usually comforting aroma smelled acrid today, turning her stomach and making her feel sick.

She sat with him as he began to eat. "I'm spoiled from having my meals cooked for me. I'll have to get used to doing it for myself again . . . for a while, that is."

He glanced into Deborah's tense face and said, "You haven't said hardly a word. Is something wrong?"

She drew a shuddering breath and said, "It's no use, Jake. After you got hurt, I realized I couldn't spend the rest of my life waiting for a bullet to take you. I'd be a wreck, worrying every day if you were going to come home. I wanted to keep my promise, but I can't. I put the ring in your bureau drawer."

She said it in such a rush that it took a moment for him to comprehend what she'd said. When he did, the shocked look on his face made her burst into tears.

"I'm sorry. I'm truly sorry."

She jumped to her feet and fled before he could follow. She didn't want to see any more of his hurt and confusion.

She didn't pause until she realized that she was running through town like a madwoman. If she didn't slow down, people were going to ask questions. And that was the last thing she wanted to face.

She forced herself to walk, hating the way other people strode down the boardwalks, smiling and exchanging greetings. It was wrong that life should go on peacefully for others while she was dying inside.

She frowned as she walked past pansies and marigolds, blooming merrily in gardens. A cold wind should be blowing instead of a warm gentle breeze. Flowers should be dormant and the trees stripped of leaves. The cold ache in her chest fit the grim iciness of winter better than the warmth and full bloom of summer.

She reached the boardinghouse and set about her chores as though she were being chased by demons. Just before lunch, Carrie called to her from the bottom of the stairs. "Come on down here. Jake wants to talk to you."

Her heart thumped painfully as she went to face him. He stood in the parlor, holding his hat and looking unhappy.

"This won't do any good, Jake. I meant what I said. We'll just drag out the torture."

"But you'd still marry me if I gave up being a sheriff?"

"Yes. But I don't know what else you'd do. I don't want you to be unhappy on account of me."

He studied her for a moment, determination replacing the pain in his eyes. "I won't try and convince you to change your mind. But I won't give up on us either."

He stayed a moment longer, neither of them saying a word. Then, hat still in hand, he said, "Good-bye, Deborah."

She felt her throat constrict as she answered, "Good-bye, Jake."

He left, closing the door softly behind him. He wouldn't try and convince her to change her mind. He'd said so. Her heart ached to think he could say good-bye so easily. Yet he'd said he wouldn't give up on them. But what chance did they have?

Tears were streaming down her cheeks when Carrie came in to say, "I couldn't help but hear what Jake said."

She took Deborah in her arms. "Oh, honey, are you sure this is the right thing to do?"

Deborah sobbed against her shoulder, at last answering, "It's the only solution. I won't wonder every day if some outlaw is going to make me a widow."

"Nothing is certain in this life, honey."

"I know. But I won't end up like Ma. Anyway, this was bad from the beginning, Carrie. Think how Jake and I started out. It was never meant to work."

Carrie shook her head. "I disagree, but I won't push you

to change your mind. But, like Jake, I won't give up hoping either."

Deborah sniffed. Jake and Carrie could hope all they liked. It wouldn't change the facts.

That afternoon, Carrie cooked up a soup and said, "Old Joe isn't feeling too well. I wonder if you'd mind taking this up to his room."

"I don't mind, though I don't think he likes me much."

Nonetheless, she took the soup and knocked on his door. She was surprised that he answered, since he'd seemed so deft. She found him lying in bed, covered with a quilt, though the afternoon was warm.

"I've brought your soup. I'm sorry you're not feeling well."

He ignored the bowl she set on the table beside him. "I've seen you and the sheriff together. Are you two getting hitched?" he asked.

"No. We were, but we've broken it off."

He patted the bed. "Sit here and tell me why."

She started to say that she had a lot of work, yet the intense interest on his face detained her. She found herself perched on the bed, telling the old man about what had happened to her ma and how she couldn't face losing Jake. She finished by saying, "It's been awful not knowing for sure what happened to Pa all these years. I thought I could come here, find out, and put it behind me, but I guess it will never be behind me."

A tear slipped down Joe's wrinkled cheek. Deborah felt touched by the old man's sensitivity. He wiped it away and said, "I have some long overdue explaining to do."

He looked her in the eyes and began. "I knew both your pas when they was working that little mine up the canyon.

I was mining, too, only my claim was a mite west of theirs. One year, just after we'd weathered the worst snowstorm of the winter, I was making my way by mule down a winding trail near Red Mountain. That's when I seen them. Actually, I seen Ed's boot."

Deborah frowned. "What do you mean?"

"They must have been walking into town to cash in their bag of silver when it caught them. The avalanche, I mean. It happens all the time. Anyway, by the time I found them, they were dead. I had a shovel on my mule, Jasper, so I dug out their bodies and buried them under the rocks to keep the animals away."

He sighed. "I didn't know about Ed's family or that Roy had a wife and son in town, not till I moved here years later. If I had, I hope I would have done the right thing and given the money right over. But by the time I moved to town, it seemed too late. And I was ashamed to admit I kept the bag of silver. I should have tried to find their kin, but my claim was bust, and I had nothing to live on. I cashed in the silver and kept the money for my provisions. I was careful and didn't spend much. It's what I've been using to pay my rent."

Deborah stared at the old man. "My father and Jake's pa were killed in an avalanche?"

Joe nodded. "I'm sorry I didn't tell sooner, but to do that meant telling about the awful thing I done. And I didn't know they had families who needed the money."

He pointed to the floor beside the small chipped bureau that held his worldly possessions. "I hollowed out the floorboard over there. Go ahead and pry it up."

Under his direction, Deborah pried up the loose board and found a small chunky bag of money in the hollow. She held it in her hand and stared at it.

Deborah felt the burden she had carried all these years
lift from her heart. She didn't have to wonder what had
happened to Pa any longer. He'd died in an act of nature.
He'd been killed, but he hadn't been murdered. There was
no foul play and no one to blame. Roy Taylor may have had
his shortcomings, but he hadn't been a killer. Deborah had
believed it for years and she'd been wrong, just like her ma
was wrong thinking Ed had run off in search of a good
time. It had made her bitter. Would the truth set her free?

"You take the money. It belongs to you, you and Jake,"
Joe said.

Deborah counted the coins. There was more than fifty
dollars in the bag. She could send Pa's half to the farm to
help with repairs.

She held it in her hand as she studied the old man.
"What would you live on?"

"I could go back to my shanty. I don't suppose it's blowed
down."

She could imagine a cold winter wind whipping through
the boards, chilling his frail body. He would huddle, ill
and alone, with no one to bring him warm soup.

She shook her head. For whatever wrong he'd done, she
couldn't sentence him to a lonely and miserable death.
That would make her as much a murderer as she'd imagined Roy to be.

"You can keep Pa's part of the money for your rent. We
won't tell Carrie where it came from. If you were suddenly
penniless, I don't expect she'd throw you out. She'd let you
stay for free. But I expect she needs this money for rent."

"You won't tell her?" His voice wobbled like a little child's.

"I won't tell her. But I will have to tell Jake. He'll have
to make his own decision about his share."

Joe nodded. "I hope he don't hate me."

Deborah replaced the money under the floorboard and stood up. She patted Joe's thin hand. "He won't hate you. Eat your soup before it gets cold."

She scurried out of Joe's room and downstairs to tell Carrie she was going out. Then she caught her hat off the hook and scurried out the door. She had to talk to Jake. What Joe had said wouldn't change things between them, but he deserved to know about his pa.

She stopped by the sheriff's office and the deputy told her Jake was out. Her spirits plunged as though a rain cloud had blocked the sun. Even though she'd broken off their engagement, she relished an excuse to see him and talk to him again. Soon, excuses would be hard to find and they would be reduced to polite nods in passing.

She trudged home with a disappointed heart.

As she entered the parlor, her pulse leaped to hear Jake talking to Pete. She paused in the doorway. Jake jumped to his feet, a grin stretching across his face. She longed to dash into his arms, to hold him and renew the magic of their love.

Instead, she forced herself to greet him. "Hello, Jake."

He continued to grin while Pete excused himself, leaving the two of them alone.

Jake looked ready to burst as he waited for her to be seated on the sofa.

He took her hands in his. "I didn't want to tell you before because I wanted to be sure I was right. The night the outlaw came to the mine, I had just stumbled on what I thought was a lode of gold. Like Red Mountain, it's in a vertical chimney instead of straight into the rock."

He paused to let the words sink in. "I was afraid of raising our hopes and finding that the lode played out. So Pete and I spent this morning blasting into the rock. And I believe we've found a sizable lode. I took a sample to Tom, and he said we're on the way to being wealthy."

Deborah knew her mouth was hanging open, yet she was powerless either to shut it or to believe what he was saying.

"You found gold?" she said at last.

"I did. Can you believe we were chipping away for bits of silver when there was a chimney full of gold all that time? Too bad for our pas that they didn't find it. They were so close. Then again, my pa would have misused it on drinking and gambling."

Deborah licked her lips. Reminded of what Joe had told her, she forced thoughts of gold from her mind and said, "Old Joe just told me that he knew what happened to our fathers. I'd gone to tell you when you came here."

She told Jake the whole story. And when she finished, he said, "Let the old man keep the money. We don't need it now. I'm relieved to know that my pa didn't murder yours. That means a lot to me."

"And to me," she said softly.

"He took her hand. You told me you'd marry me if I quit being a sheriff. How would you like being married to a rancher? For a long time, it's been my dream to buy land up near Colona. I talked it over with Red Deer. He's willing to bring his family there and help run the ranch. We'll have enough money from the value of our land and cattle that you'd never have to worry about being left alone and poor."

"I think I would love being married to a rancher. And I'd like being neighbors with Morning Star."

"Then the wedding is back on?"

She blinked back tears of happiness. "It's back on. I won't worry about you chasing cows instead of outlaws. Cows don't shoot straight."

He hooted and pulled her into his arms.

Carrie came scurrying into the room. "What's all the racket?"

"Dust out your cake pans," Jake said. "The wedding's back on."

Carrie let out a whoop and said, "Pete told me about the gold. I guess our town will be looking for a new sheriff."

"It certainly will," said Deborah, her lashes sparkling with her tears.

Then she wondered out loud, "Who's going to look after the mine while we're off running a ranch?"

"Why, Pete, of course. He's going to hire workers and take care of the day-to-day operations for a share of the profit."

"Everything has worked out perfectly," Deborah said. She grinned slyly. "Just think. When we move off, Oscar won't have you to criticize anymore."

Carrie shook her head. "Oscar quit picking on Jake and started in on the mayor. His boss had enough and fired him yesterday. Oscar's packing his bags to leave town."

"I hope he's not coming to Colona," Deborah said.

Jake gave a low husky growl and pulled her into his lap. "Forget Oscar."

He opened his fist and dangled the wedding ring in front of her. "Will you take this back now?"

She smiled. "I will. And I'll never take it off again."

Carrie sniffed as she watched Jake place the chain around Deborah's neck. "I'll get Pete and bring some wine, and we'll celebrate."

Jake leaned over and kissed Deborah.

She snuggled against him, feeling their hearts beat as one. "I've never been so happy in my whole life."

He ran his finger gently down her cheek and said, "Believe me, my love, the best is yet to come."

And with a heart overflowing with love, Deborah could at last believe that it was true.